LAWFULLY MATCHED

A TEXAS LAWKEEPER ROMANCE

LORANA HOOPES

COPYRIGHT

This book is dedicated to all the hardworking law enforcement officers out there. Our world would not be as safe without all of you.

And to my family who lets me sacrifice time with them to write these stories in my head.

NOTE FROM THE AUTHOR

Thank you so much for picking up this book. I hope you enjoy the story and the characters as they are dear to my heart. If you do, please leave a review at your retailer. It really does make a difference because it lets people make an informed decision about books. Below are the other books in this series. I would love for you to check them out. I'd also like to offer you a sample of my newest book. Free Sample!

Lawkeepers series:
Lawfully Justified

The Scarlet Wedding

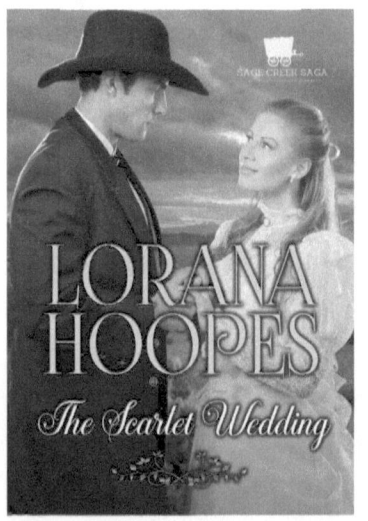

Lawfully Redeemed

Lawfully Pursued

CHAPTER ONE

B oston, Massachusetts 1883

MARY KATHERINE WHIDBY grabbed the local paper and strolled to a corner to read in private. While she hated to leave her beloved Boston, she was quickly approaching the spinster age, and all the surrounding men seemed intimidated by her brains or more likely her strong-willed spirit as her brother Robert liked to remind her.

Mary Katherine, or Kate as her family called her, had always held a grand notion of love, so agreeing to marry a complete stranger caused distaste in her mouth every time she thought about it, but her options had run out when her parents died.

She opened the paper and scanned the offerings:

'Forty-year-old widowed rancher looking for wife who can be a mother to three kids.'

Three kids? Kate shook her head and drew a line through that one. While she wanted kids one day, she did not feel confident stepping into the role immediately.

'Fifty-year-old Pastor seeks wife for companionship and to lead women's socials at local church.'

A pastor's wife wouldn't be too bad, but the age difference was more than Kate could stomach. After all, she was barely twenty-five, which would make this man twice her age, and wasn't the lifespan shorter in the west? Knowing her luck, he would die shortly after she arrived, and she'd be left all alone.

'Thirty-year-old saloon owner seeks wife and possible waitress.'

While this one was closer in age, Kate had no desire, or skills for that matter, to work in a saloon.

The pickings were slim this month it seemed. Just one ad left.

'Thirty-two-year-old farmer in search of brave woman to help on homestead.'

Well, she didn't know much about farming, but no

one would say Kate wasn't brave. She had even taken shooting lessons with her brother and father.

Crossing her fingers this man would not be a con man or an abuser, she made her way to the counter.

"Hello Miss Kate, what can I help you with today?" Mr. Gaines, the elderly owner of the newspaper asked. He wore a black vest over his shirt and a pair of old spectacles sat on the bridge of his nose.

Kate cleared her throat, still embarrassed to be doing this. "I wanted to inquire how I might go about answering an ad."

"Hmm, let me see," he said, pushing up his glasses as he read the ad. "Mail-order bride?" He looked up at Kate. "Does that mean we're losing you?"

A heated flush flared across Kate's face. "Well, there isn't much left for me here with mother and father gone."

"Don't you still have a brother?" Mr. Gaines asked kindly.

Kate nodded. "I do, but Robert just married, and he's trying to get his practice up and running. I would just be in the way." She didn't add the fact that his wife Abigail appeared to despise her, and the thought of staying in their house much longer held little appeal.

"Well, if you're sure," he said, though the tone of his voice told her he wasn't convinced. He reached below the cabinet and pulled out a pad of paper and a pencil. "Generally, you write the man back and see if it's a good fit."

"Oh," Kate stammered. She had not realized she would need to reply. "Thank you," she said taking the paper and pencil. "I will return this shortly."

Kate headed back to the corner and sat down at the table, thinking for a moment. She placed the pencil on the paper and scribbled out:

DEAR MR. EASTERLY,

My name is Kate Whidby. I am a brave twenty-five-year-old woman with dark hair and blue eyes. I am looking for love and adventure in a new area. I saw your ad in my paper, and although I do not know much about farming, I am a quick study and think I could be the woman you are looking for. Please advise if this is acceptable. I would like to travel as soon as possible.

Kate Whidby

SHE FOLDED the letter and returned to Mr. Gaines. "Do you have an envelope I could use to send this?"

Mr. Gaines supplied one from under the counter and handed it to her. Kate quickly jotted her name and address down and sealed the envelope. She held it out to Mr. Gaines, but he shook his head.

"Take it to the post office. They will send it out and your response will come back through them."

"How long do you think it will take to get a reply?"

"I don't know for sure, but my guess would be about two weeks."

Kate's jaw dropped open. "Two weeks?"

Mr. Gaines nodded and scratched the side of his bald head with the back of the pencil. "Yes ma'am, unless you'd like to telegraph it. That costs considerably more though."

Kate fingered the few coins she had managed to find in her parent's bedroom as she was packing up the last items she'd been able to take. No, she had better be frugal and spend only a little.

"No, two weeks is fine." Perhaps, she could find a temporary job. It would be nice to have some money for the trip.

Kate paid the small fee and left with the letter in hand. After a quick stop in the post office to drop it off, she continued on to the mercantile to pick up a few items.

Once inside the store, she loaded the basket with the necessities—flour, sugar, teas—and then picked up a few pieces of penny candy. Kate felt guilty for imposing on Robert and Abigail by staying with them at their house, especially so early in their marriage, but her parents had rented their house. Kate took care for her parents but had no money to continue the payments after their death, and so she had been forced to give up her home.

"Morning, Miss Kate," Sally, the plump owner of the Mercantile, smiled at her.

Kate had often wondered how Sally had married before she did, but then she would remember the two marriage proposals she had turned down. Funny how she had rebuffed those proposals because she felt she didn't know the men well enough, yet now she was planning to travel across the country and marry a man she'd never met.

"Hello, Sally," she said, laying the items on the counter. "How is business?"

"It is not too bad," Sally said. Then she glanced behind her and leaned forward. "Tell you the truth, it has been a little slow the last few months. John is stressed about it," she whispered.

Kate smiled and leaned in to reply. "Well, I will keep praying it will pick up."

"That is mighty kind of you, Kate. Will I see you at church on Sunday?"

Kate nodded, but the question sent her mind spinning. God was an important part of her life. Would there be proper churches in Texas?

∼

SAGE CREEK, Texas 1883

JESSE JENNINGS REMOVED his hat and wiped the sweat from his brow. Finally, the last fence post was in. With his cattle safe once again, he would now be able to focus on putting the finishing touches on his homestead, so he could marry Pauline.

As he replaced his hat, Sheriff Johnson rode up. Jesse sighed and lifted his gaze to the lawman.

"What can I do for you, Sheriff?" he asked, though he knew the answer to the question. Sheriff Johnson had come around once every few days like clockwork over the past month, trying to enlist Jessie as a deputy sheriff.

Jesse enjoyed the protection the law provided as much as the next person, but he was just a simple rancher, and all he wanted to do was marry his sweetheart and raise cattle.

Unfortunately, time and money had dwindled after some rough winter weather and the previous summer's drought, extending the finishing of the homestead.

"You know why I'm here, Jesse," the older man said as he dismounted his chocolate brown stallion. "There was another robbery last night. This time at Doc Moore's office. No one was hurt, but they took a lot of his supplies. We need more men to help patrol. At least until we catch these varmints." He removed his hat and ran his leathery hand through his salt-and-pepper hair.

"I'm sorry to hear that Sheriff, but as I've told you before, I'm not a lawman, and I need to finish this homestead."

Sheriff Johnson planted his hands on his slim hips and donned his hat again. "Well, I can set with that, but the attacks appear to be becoming more frequent. I just hope you still have a home when all is said and done."

With that, Sheriff Johnson tipped the brim of his black Stetson before re-mounting his horse.

Jesse lifted a hand in a loose wave and watched the sheriff recede from view. Maybe Sheriff Johnson was right. He was young, in shape, and not half bad with a gun.

Once he finished the homestead he'd be able to think about it. Right now, thoughts of Pauline with her long blonde hair consumed his thoughts.

Jesse checked the sun on the horizon. It had sunk low, leaving the sky a brilliant orange and pink color. He had lost track of time and needed to wash up before dinner with his fiancée.

CHAPTER TWO

"You did what?" Robert asked over dinner that night.

"I answered a mail-order bride ad," Kate repeated as she scooped mashed potatoes on her plate.

"You cannot go halfway across the country to marry a man you've never met," Robert said, slamming his hand against the table with enough force to send the cutlery dancing.

Kate bit the inside of her lip to calm her words before speaking. Robert was a year younger than she was, but he had tried to step into her father's role since their parents' death.

"I do not have much choice," Kate said. "I turned down the few marriage proposals I had, and there have not been any more."

"And what was wrong with those men?" Robert asked.

"Well, one was a lecherous man nearly twice my age, and the other was not a Christian," Kate returned.

"Perhaps if you engaged in proper activities like other women do, there might be more," Robert said with a pointed look in her direction.

"I think it is a wonderful idea," Abigail said with fake sincerity from the end of the table. "Goodness knows we can barely afford to feed another mouth around here." Her disingenuous smile melted away as she shot Kate a disapproving look.

"I don't like it," Robert said, ignoring the insult his wife had sent Kate's direction. "What if this man turns out to be a lecher or some other kind of ruffian?"

"I seriously doubt that type of man would advertise in the newspaper," Kate said, taking a sip of her tea, "but as for the rest, I will have to leave that in God's hands."

Robert opened his mouth to argue further, but Kate had stopped him with her trusting God comment. It was something neither of them were very good at, but which Kate had resolved to be better.

"When will you know?" Robert asked with resignation in his voice.

"Mr. Gaines said it would take about two weeks to get a reply," Kate said.

"Well, then I will use that time to pray this isn't God's will, and that the man will find someone else," Robert said as he reached for another piece of chicken.

"Fine," Kate agreed. "But if he answers yes, you will have to let me go."

"Agreed." Robert ended the conversation with a curt nod.

Kate dropped her hands to her lap and folded them together in a nervous gesture. "Do you know of anyone looking for short term work?" she asked, glancing up at him before returning her eyes to her lap. "I would like to save up a little more before making the trip."

"For a trip you are not even sure you are making yet?" Robert's volume had risen again and the vein at the base of his neck bulged as it often did when he grew angry.

"The school is looking for someone," Abigail spoke up. The quick suggestion wasn't surprising since Kate was certain the other woman would be grateful to get rid of her during the day. "One of the regular teachers was forced to take a few weeks to visit an ailing family member. I am sure even you could handle teaching for a couple of weeks."

It wasn't surprising Abigail ended her suggestion with a jab at Kate's capability. Her sister-in-law took every opportunity to shine a light on her shortcomings—real or imagined.

Even though she had her misgivings about Abigail's motives, Kate mulled the prospect over in her mind. While she wasn't formally educated, she had pored over Robert's books and taught herself a great deal. Surely, teaching a few students wouldn't be too hard for a week or so.

"I THINK you should think about it," Pauline said as she spooned soup into Jesse's bowl. "I've heard the robberies have been getting more frequent, and the sheriff could use more good men."

"I agree," her mother, Iris, said from the stove where she was pulling out bread to go with dinner. "Your father said he heard tell of another stagecoach getting robbed in Opdyke West. That's not far from here, and the whole business makes me nervous."

Jesse grabbed Pauline's hand as her mother turned back to the stove. "If I become a deputy, it will mean delaying the homestead even more. I want it to be finished for when we marry, and I have a hankering to be married already."

Pauline brushed a lock of hair behind his ear. "We've waited this long, Jesse Jennings. We can wait a little longer. Besides, I would feel guilty moving into our nice, new home while other people's houses and businesses are still being attacked."

Jesse smiled and shook his head. "That is why I love you, Pauline Masterson. You have such a good heart." Jesse tugged on her hand to bring her closer, so he could take in her sweet smell, but she pushed him away and crossed to her chair.

"We are not going to let this soup get cold, Jesse," she said playfully. "I worked too hard on it."

"Yes ma'am," Jesse said, nodding his head and placing his napkin on his lap. "I would sure hate for anything you make to go to waste."

A soft pink color tinged Pauline's fair cheek as she sat across from him.

"Well, it should just be another minute," Iris said as she placed the bread on the table.

The cabin door banged open and Pauline's father, Caleb, and her brother, James, entered.

"You weren't about to start without us, were you?" James was tall and beefy, and his frame filled the doorway. Pauline's father was slightly shorter, but nearly as broad shouldered.

"No, we were waiting," Pauline said. "I just dished the stew, so it should still be warm."

"Yes, come and sit," her mother said.

"I'm sorry we're late," James said, limping into the

large room that served as the main living space. "It takes me longer to finish chores now since my accident." James had the habit of frequenting the saloon a little too often, and a skirmish one night had ended with shots fired. One had hit his foot, shattering the bone.

"It looks as though your foot is healing though," Jesse said as James made it to the table and fell into the chair to his right. Her father took the chair to Jesse's left.

"Humph," James mumbled through a mouthful of soup. He had not waited to pray but had simply dug into the meal.

"Well, let's not let the food get cold," Pauline's mother said, ignoring James's slurping and picking up her own spoon.

Jesse lowered his head to say a silent prayer and then smiled at Pauline, who had done the same. The rest of her family often forgot to pray at meals, but he and Pauline never missed the opportunity.

Jesse could not wait until they were married, and it could be just her and him at every meal. Though James and her parents served as decent chaperones, they made less than stellar dinner companions.

The rest of the dinner passed in an uncomfortable silence, and Jesse found himself relieved when it ended.

After Pauline and her mother had cleaned the dishes, Jesse gathered his things to go, and Pauline walked him to the front door. Jesse reached for her hand, but a cough from James forced him to drop it back to his side. Jesse wanted to take her in his arms and feel her soft lips against his, but if holding hands was frowned upon, that would definitely have to wait a little longer.

"Goodnight Pauline," he said with a bow. "I look forward to another meal tomorrow." Jesse's family was no longer living, but Pauline's family had been kind enough to offer him a chair for dinner each night.

"I do as well," she said and smiled sweetly at him.

CHAPTER THREE

Kate collapsed into the chair behind the desk and sighed. Teaching was a lot harder than she had imagined. There were twenty-three children in her class and most were boys. They had assigned her the primary grades, and although she had a curriculum, she spent more of her time dealing with classroom management than she often did instructing. It was exhausting work, both mentally and physically.

At least today was Friday. That gave her two whole days to relax before school opened again on Monday. She took one more deep breath and gathered up her papers and books. If she were lucky, she would have just enough time to check at the post office about her response before it closed.

She had adopted the habit of stopping by the post

office on the way home, but tonight the boys had been particularly feisty, and school had run late. Kate locked the schoolroom door and tucked the key in the pocket of her blue cotton dress before setting out.

Normally, Mr. Prescott, who worked the afternoon shift, would shake his head as she entered the post office, and she would smile and try to hide her disappointment, but today he was waiting for her at the door. As soon as he saw her approaching, his eyes lit up, and he gestured for her to follow him inside. Kate quickened her pace, excited to see what her future held.

Mr. Prescott was at the back counter when she followed him through the office. He held a white envelope in his hands. "An envelope came today, Miss Kate."

Kate was surprised to see her hand shaking as she reached for the envelope. She thought she had made peace with whatever the decision would be, but suddenly her mouth went dry and her heart was beating erratically in her chest.

She turned the envelope over and slid one finger under the seal. The paper seemed to tear in slow motion, and a folded piece of paper poked out. Kate pulled it out, unfolded it, and scanned the words.

Dear Ms. Whidby

I would be delighted to have you come to Lisbon, Texas to

be my wife. You sound like a woman who could handle herself in the West. I have enclosed a ticket for the third Friday in April. I look forward to meeting you soon.

Bill Easterly

"Did you receive what you were hoping for?" Mr. Prescott didn't know the entire story, but Kate figured he must be curious about her daily visits.

"He said yes. I suppose I am moving to Texas." Kate had thought she would feel excitement at the news, but the only emotion she could pinpoint was shock. Perhaps she should have corresponded more with him, but her uncomfortable living situation had hastened the process. "Thank you, Mr. Prescott," she said, re-folding the paper and tucking it in her pocket beside the school key.

"Best of luck," Mr. Prescott called as she headed toward the entrance in a daze.

"Thank you," she said.

The third Friday in April was the end of next week. She would have just one more week with her brother and four more days with the students. Suddenly, the impending move felt too fast, but there was no turning back now.

JESSE LOOKED up from where he was patching holes in

the barn as the thundering of hoofprints approached. *What in the world?* He wasn't expecting company, and it was nearly lunchtime, which was an odd time for someone to visit. His hand moved to the hilt of his Colt revolver, but before he had time to pull it out, a shot whizzed by his ear. He dropped to the ground and scanned the area. Why was someone shooting at him?

Seconds later, three horses carrying masked men flew past him. From his position on the ground, Jesse aimed and fired. The first shot went wide, but he rolled up on his knee and focused for the second shot. It didn't knock the rider from his horse, but he heard the man's yelp as they disappeared in a cloud of dust. Jesse wondered if these men were the ones who had been robbing Sage Creek and the surrounding towns.

He raced to his horse, Molly, who was tied up a few yards away, but before he could mount her, two more horses and riders arrived.

Pastor Lewis, along with his son, Theodore, approached with sullen looks on their faces.

"What are you doing here, Pastor?" Jesse inquired.

"You best come back to town with us, Jesse," Pastor Lewis stated.

A feeling of dread like a bucket loaded down with rocks filled Jesse's insides. "Why? What happened?"

"They were robbing the bank, Jesse," Theodore answered.

Jesse shook his head, still not comprehending.

"Pauline was in the bank making a deposit for her wedding dress and was hit when Josiah and the men exchanged fire," Theodore said.

"Is Pauline alright?" Jesse's words felt tight, strangled in his throat.

"She's at Doc Moore's," Pastor Lewis stated.

Jesse did not wait to follow the other men back. Instead, he gave Molly a swift kick, something he rarely did, and led the charge himself back to town. Jesse had opted to live on the outskirts of town, so he would have more land to ranch, but he cursed that decision now as the minutes ticked by.

When he finally reached the clinic, Jesse jumped off Molly and threw her reins around the hitching post in one deft movement before mounting the steps and throwing the door to the clinic open.

Doc Moore—an elderly man with a full head of white hair—looked up as he entered. The doctor sat near the bed, where Pauline was laid out, her blonde hair streaked with red from a wound in her temple.

"Pauline." The word was barely more than a whisper as Jesse crossed the distance and fell to his knees before her. He picked up her hand, surprised to find it still warm. Jesse turned his question-filled eyes on Doc Moore.

"She's resting right now," Doc Moore said. "The

wound on her temple was just a graze of a stray bullet. It's the one that hit her stomach that's the problem."

Pauline's eyes slowly opened, but they were not the same green Jesse was used to seeing. They had faded to a dull gray and appeared cloudy. She tried to smile, but the effort sent her coughing and a trickle of red ran out of her mouth. Jesse grabbed the handkerchief from his pocket and wiped the blood away.

"I'm glad you're here, Jesse," she said in a raspy voice.

"Don't try to talk," Jesse said, sniffing back tears as he caressed her hair.

"I don't have long," she said and coughed again, "but I wanted to tell you that one of the men has a scar on the back of his hand. A half-moon."

Jesse nodded. "I'll find him, Pauline. I will."

She shook her head. "Don't look for vengeance, Jesse. Protect the town." A deep cough shook her body, and another, larger stream of blood flowed out of her mouth. "Remember that I love you."

"I love you too," Jesse said, but his words were too late. He could almost see the life leave Pauline as her eyes turned glassy and remained fixed on a point past his shoulder.

"No," Jesse cried out and placed his forehead on Pauline's forearm. "No!"

"I'm sorry, Jesse," Doc Moore said, patting his

shoulder. "There was nothing I could do but make her comfortable."

Jesse didn't bother looking up. With his face hidden, he could let the tears flow and the rage build. The doctor stayed by his side another few minutes, but finally he heard the man stand and move to another room to give him some privacy.

"I will avenge your death, Pauline," Jesse whispered to the woman he had loved for the last year. "I will find the men who did this, and they will pay."

Jesse ran a rough hand across his eyes and pushed himself up from the bedside. With a single-minded focus, he strode across the room and flung the front door open. Sheriff Johnson and one of the deputies stood on the porch, their hats in their hands.

"Make me a deputy today," Jesse said, his voice cold and flat. "They will not strike here again."

CHAPTER FOUR

K ate stood on the train platform, a bundle of nerves. Her toiletries were packed in her carpetbag, which she gripped tightly in her hand. Her mother's wedding dress, shoes, her other clothes, and a few other sentimental items were packed in her trunk, which was already on the train.

"Are you sure you want to do this?" Robert asked. Worry lines marred his forehead and his hazel eyes were filled with concern. "You can stay with us as long as it takes, Kate."

Kate glanced at Abigail who while smiling still had the ability to hold Kate in a cold stare of disapproval. "That is kind of you, Robert," she said, returning her attention to him, "but I feel this is where God is leading me. I will not deny I am a little apprehensive, but I believe he will protect and provide for me."

"You better write," Robert said as he pulled her in for a fierce hug.

Kate would miss pieces of Boston, like the library and the stables. She doubted the West would have an expansive library like Boston did, and she would miss riding through the park after church. In fact, the West probably wouldn't have some of the finer amenities she was used to, but more than those, she would miss Robert. They had been distant growing up, but after the death of their parents, they had become closer.

She would not, however, miss the insulting comments from Abigail or the cool stares often passed her direction during meal times.

"Of course I will," Kate said, emotion constricting her throat. She had not expected leaving to be so hard. Even quitting the school had been more emotional than she had expected. While the older boys had not seemed to care she was leaving, one of the younger boys had run up and hugged her legs. Surprised, she had patted his hair, promising him their regular teacher would be returning soon.

"All aboard." The shout from the train conductor ended Kate's memory of the day before.

"I suppose I should be going," Kate said with a sigh. "I will write as soon as I arrive." Before Robert could say anything further, Kate hurried onto the train. She chose a seat at a window and waved to them.

Moments later the train surged forward as it pulled out of the station.

"Is this seat taken?"

Kate looked up to see an older woman clad all in black looking down at her.

"No, it's available," Kate said, picking up her bag and holding it on her lap.

"Thank you," the woman said as she sat. "I have not traveled by train before, and I must admit I am a little nervous."

"Me too." Kate offered her seatmate a small smile.

"Oh, wonderful. Then we can try it out together," the woman said. "I only wish I were traveling under different circumstances."

"Oh?" Kate didn't want to pry, but the woman had brought it up.

"Yes, unfortunately I am heading out West due to a death in my family. Well, two actually. My husband passed away two months ago, and after my grand-daughter was killed in a bank robbery, I decided to move out West to be close to the only family I have left."

Kate's eyes widened, and her hand shot to her open mouth. "I am so sorry for your loss."

"Me too," the woman said. "Charles was older and had lived a full life, but Pauline was so young, only twenty years of age and about to be married."

"Oh, that's awful," Kate murmured. She felt bad for her seatmate and for the poor woman's family, but she was also more worried about her own safety now. Kate had known the West might be dangerous, but she had never thought about bank robberies.

"I am sorry for going on," the woman said. "You did not ask for my sad story. My name is Ellen by the way, what is your name, dear?"

"My name is Kate."

Ellen smiled at her. "Nice to meet you, Kate. What are you heading West for?"

"I am heading West to get married," Kate said softly and then bit her lip. Normally marriage was a happy occasion, but she felt bad discussing hers with this woman as her granddaughter had been about to marry.

Ellen appeared to take no offense to this statement. "That is wonderful, dear. I know I enjoyed my years with Charles. I wish you the best of luck."

As the train chugged westward, the two women continued to chat and share their stories. Kate was glad to have made a friend even if it was only until they reached Texas.

JESSE LOOKED down at the star on his shirt and shook

his head. It did not feel very different, and there had been no big ceremony—just the sheriff asking him if he promised to protect the town and him agreeing. The other deputy had stood in as a witness, and in a matter of minutes, the ceremony was over, and Jesse was a deputy.

"Now can we go after Pauline's killers?" he asked the other men.

"No, Jesse," the sheriff said. "We don't know where these men are. We must protect the town here, at least until we have an idea of where to go. Then we can form a posse and go after them."

Jesse wanted to argue. He wanted to tear out of the room, mount Molly, and go in search of the robbers himself, but as he looked at the other men in the room, he realized they also had people important in their lives—wives and sons and daughters. As much as he wanted to avenge Pauline's death, he also did not want anyone else feeling the pain he did at this moment.

"Fine," he said with a sigh and a mental promise to never stop searching for the men responsible on his own time. "What do we do now then?"

"We take turns patrolling," Jeb Greene, the other deputy said. He had salt and pepper streaks through his hair and a weathered face to match. Jeb was one of the Greene brothers who had been part of the original settlement of the town.

"That sounds fine," Jesse said with a curt nod. "Where should I patrol?"

"We have a rotation," the sheriff said, pointing to a scribbled list on the wall. "One person stays here to watch any prisoners and be ready in case anyone in town needs help. The other two patrol the town borders. We lost Josiah yesterday in the bank robbery, but with the addition of you, there are still three of us."

Jesse glanced at the other men. In his grief over Pauline, he had forgotten Josiah had been killed as well, and these men were probably upset too.

"Jeb, why don't you take Jesse and show him the patrol route?" the sheriff continued. "I will hold down the fort here."

Jesse nodded, though he wondered if there were a better way as the patrols yesterday hadn't stopped the robbery or the killings from happening. He followed Jeb out to where their horses were tied up.

With a swift motion, he untied the reins and then swung up and mounted Molly, who had been a gift from his mother the summer before she died. Pale and sickly, his mother had never fully adjusted to the rigor of the West and had caught a fever ten years ago and never recovered. While his father had been broken, Jesse had been even more so and when he was old enough, he had left the small town in east Texas and traveled further west, stopping in Sage

Creek when he found a job and a possibility of owning his own land.

After a year of working with a rancher on the outskirts of town, mending his fences and wrangling his cattle, he had earned enough to buy a small piece of land of his own. A year later he had met Pauline. Pauline, who without knowing it, had inspired him to start his own ranch. It hadn't been easy, but he now had enough livestock to make a decent living. Unfortunately, he no longer had Pauline to share that life with.

"It isn't a perfect system," Jeb said as he led the way out of town, "but we ride in a slow circle around the town, paying closest attention to the road to Lisbon and the road from Belleville as that is where this pack of bandits seems to come from most often. Yesterday, we rode together, but after what happened, I am going to suggest we each take half of the perimeter. Perhaps that will make it harder for them to sneak past us."

"Alright," Jesse said. He knew the likelihood of the men hitting again today was small, but he hoped they would be stupid enough to try it and that he'd be the one they crossed.

JESSE SAT in the far corner of the saloon that night nursing a beer. He rarely drank and never frequented the saloon, but since losing Pauline yesterday, he felt lost. The patrol today had been uneventful, and while Jesse was glad to not have more violence, he could not help feeling the need to be doing something more to avenge Pauline.

"Sorry about your loss, hon."

Jesse looked up to see a buxom blond standing over his table. Her bright red corset was cinched tight with black laces to create the illusion of a thinner waist, but all it did was send extra skin spilling over the top. Jesse dropped his eyes. These scantily clad women were only one reason he had generally avoided saloons.

"Thank you," he mumbled into his mug.

"I could help you forget your pain," she said in a suggestive voice as her hand touched his arm.

Jesse flung her arm away and stood up. "Don't touch me." The room tilted and spun as he tried to focus. Somewhere in the midst of the swaying, he saw the girl cower back before the long-haired owner rushed to her side.

"What's the problem, Lizzie?" the owner growled. Clad entirely in black with dark eyes and a scar on his cheek, the man was a fearsome sight even when he wasn't angry, but when irritated, his face grew red and mottled, reminding Jesse of a bull about to charge. The normally noisy establishment was now silent, watching the scene unfold, and undoubtedly waiting for a fight to breakout. Though Jesse had never participated, he had often heard the men of the town talk about the entertainment of fights at the saloon.

"It was my fault, Wyatt," the woman said. Though still quiet, her voice held a firm resolve. "He just lost his fiancée, and I pushed him when I shouldn't have."

Wyatt turned to Jesse who was leaning against the wall, trying to keep from getting sick. Alcohol was another reason he didn't frequent saloons. He never had learned to like the taste, and he hated what it did to his stomach.

"I think it is time you left for tonight," Wyatt said. "I don't like my ladies getting upset."

"I was just leaving anyway," Jesse slurred. He pulled a few coins from his pocket and tossed them on the table before staggering out of the saloon.

He should never have been in there, not as a Christian and not now that he was a deputy. It did not create the type of image he wanted to portray, and it didn't make him feel any better; but with Pauline gone, his life was suddenly upside down, and he no longer knew which way was up. Even worse, he wasn't sure that he cared.

He had almost made it to his horse when something caught his foot and he stumbled, falling onto the dusty ground. For a minute, he thought about simply laying his head down and sleeping off his stupor there, but before he could, a hand appeared in front of his face. Jesse raised his eyes to see Pastor Lewis staring down at him.

"I was hoping to find you, Jesse," the pastor said. His soft, kind voice usually uplifted Jesse's spirits, but tonight Jesse didn't want pity. He just wanted the pain to stop.

"Why, Pastor? Why did he take her?"

The pastor took Jesse's hand and helped him stand. "We can't always see God's plan, but he has one, Jesse, and we have to trust that good will come even in the midst of our trials."

CHAPTER FIVE

K ate rubbed her eyes as the sunlight streamed through the window opposite her. She wanted to roll over and fall back to sleep, but every part of her body ached from the hard, wooden bed.

"Good morning, Kate. How did you sleep?"

Ah, yes, Ellen was the inconsiderate neighbor who had lifted her shade at whatever ungodly hour it was. "Not as well as I'd hoped," Kate said, pushing herself into a seated position. "How do people travel on these things for days on end? I need a decent bed and a washing in the worst way."

Ellen smiled. "I suppose when you have lived as long as I have, you will have slept on a myriad of beds, some more comfortable than others. I find I can sleep almost anywhere now because of it."

"Did you move often?" Kate asked. She had only ever lived in the house with her parents and then the house with Robert and both had been of adequate standards. They might not have been rich, but they had actual beds and wash basins that were filled daily.

"Well, I was born in England. We moved to the Americas when I was about twenty-five. Unfortunately, my husband had a hard time finding work, and we were forced to move a few times until he could find a steady job. I didn't mind it as much, but my daughter never adjusted to the multiple moves, and when she was old enough, she moved West with her husband in hopes of finding a permanent home. I have only been out there once before, but she seemed happy."

"I thought you said this was your first time on a train," Kate said, confused.

Ellen laughed and sat next to Kate. "That is true. The last time I went, I had to make the whole journey by stagecoach. It was a long journey, and I much prefer the train."

"How long did it take by stagecoach?" Kate asked.

"Weeks," Ellen said with a smile. "And while I'll still have to take a stagecoach to get to Sage Creek, it will be a much shorter journey this time. I do believe there is a wash basin on board if you would like to venture with me to find it."

"I would love that," Kate said as she touched her

hair. It was no longer in the position she had placed it yesterday before leaving, and she felt grimy.

As the other passengers in the sleeping car began to stir, the two women made their way down the aisle in search of a place to clean up.

JESSE STOOD a respectful distance from the gravesite. Though he wanted to be up front, after all Pauline had nearly been his wife, James had made it abundantly clear that Jesse was neither wanted nor welcome up front with the family. And so he stood, with his hat in his hands at the back, feeling very much like an outsider.

"Pauline's life was taken far too early," Pastor Lewis said from the front. "But we have to remember that God has a plan for everything. We often do not know why things happen, but He does. Remember that He knows of every hair on your head, and He has a purpose for everything He allows to happen. That does not mean we cannot mourn Pauline, for she was a dear sister, daughter, and friend to all of us, but we know that she is in a better place with no suffering and pain. For that we can rejoice."

He paused and looked out over the small crowd gathered. "Is there anyone who would like to say a word on Pauline's behalf? Or share a story from memory?"

Jesse wanted to barge his way to the front. He had so many memories of Pauline. The way she smiled at him when he entered a room. The way her laugh sounded musical like the bells they sometimes played in church at Christmas. Or the way her hand felt like the finest silk, but no one wanted to hear these memories. And if he were honest, Jesse didn't want to share them. He wanted to tuck his memories inside and hold them close to his heart.

When Rebecca, Pauline's childhood friend, stepped forward, Jesse knew it was time for him to go. There was nothing more he could do here and listening to other people's memories of Pauline wouldn't fill the hole in his heart.

Glad for once he was at the back, Jesse slipped quietly away from the grave site. He had tied Molly up to a tree out of sight, and he headed that direction. She was happily munching on some grass when he approached; blissfully unaware of the surrounding sadness.

As he rode back to his homestead, Jesse wondered about his future. Of course, he would do nothing until he avenged her death, but after that, what? He had stayed in Sage Creek for Pauline. With her gone, should he pull up roots and find a new home?

KATE WAS ESPECIALLY glad she had made a friend in Ellen when the train pulled into the final station and they were forced to switch to the stage coach. Though it was her first time as well, Ellen seemed to know what to do and who to talk to in order to make sure their trunks were pulled off the train and loaded onto the correct stagecoach. It made Kate wonder if there were some book she should have read before making the trip.

"How do you know how to do all of this?" Kate asked as her curiosity got the better of her.

Ellen laughed as she gathered her bag. "I asked a friend who made a trip a few months ago. I figured the process could not have changed that much in that short amount of time though it feels like technology is changing every day. One day I believe we will have some form of transportation even faster than a train."

"That would be something," Kate agreed, "though I cannot see how it would work. Even trains are expensive. How would we ever afford something faster?"

"Well, that is what I said about trains before they became more prevalent but look at me now."

Kate nodded and followed Ellen off the train and to the platform where their trunks had been unloaded.

"Where would you ladies like these taken?" the porter asked them.

"You can place them over at the stagecoach office," Ellen said, handing him a few coins and pointing to a smaller building off to the left that had a similar platform to the train station.

"Yes ma'am," the man said and began hefting their trunks toward the building.

"Shall we check in?" Ellen asked.

Kate nodded, but her attention was focused on the town around her. It was very different from Boston. Everything was brown and there were not as many trees. While there were buildings, they were all single stories whereas some of the buildings back home were several stories tall.

"Kate? Are you coming?" Ellen asked, placing a black gloved hand on Kate's arm.

"Oh, yes, sorry," Kate stammered. "I was just struck by how different it is here." She followed Ellen to the stagecoach office where Ellen purchased her ticket and Kate redeemed the pass she had been sent.

"Well, it looks like we have a few minutes before the coach arrives," Ellen said. "Would you like to walk around?"

Kate nodded. Her body was not used to being in an enclosed space for such a long time. "Where might we go to look at fabric? I'd like to see what the styles are out here as I have the feeling I will be overdressed."

"Nonsense," Ellen said, placing her hands on her hips. "The women here aren't that far behind us. Maybe they don't bustle, but otherwise your dresses will be similar, though probably of a nicer fabric. However, I do love seeing the latest fashions myself, and I bet the Mercantile will have what we are looking for."

She led the way across the dusty road and into the shop. Kate was surprised how much smaller it was than her fabric shop in Boston. The one back home was two stories and held all sorts of fabrics laid out with enough space in between that you could see each one. This shop had maybe a quarter of the selection and all the fabric was jammed together to fit in the shop.

"Can I help you find anything?" A blond woman with her hair pulled back in a knot at the nape of her neck approached them. Her grey Calico dress was simple with no bustle at the back, but it did have a row of lace around the collar and at the bottom of the sleeves.

"We are just looking to see what the current fabric might be," Ellen said.

"We just received some lovely velvet and satin in," the woman said, leading the way to the fabric closest to the window. "This is what most women are wearing in the winter. I know it's a little early, but it never hurts to be prepared."

Kate admired the dark green and sapphire blue colors of the velvet and satin fabrics as the woman continued.

"Of course, we also have some lovely cotton that just came in. This herringbone was especially popular for outerwear this last year."

"Thank you," Ellen said. "Might we spend some time looking around?"

The woman nodded. "My name is Mary. If you need anything, just holler."

"Do you sew?" Ellen asked Kate as Mary walked away.

Kate dropped her eyes. "I do, but I am not very accomplished. I preferred riding to sitting in a house sewing. My mother made most of my dresses or hired the local seamstress in town. Do they have seamstresses out here?"

"I'm sure they do," Ellen said, "but I imagine you will find sewing to be a necessary skill. You had best find a tutor when you can."

The women spent the next hour looking through the shop, and Ellen purchased some of the deep purple velvet. Kate wanted to purchase some as well, but she had no idea what else she might have to buy and therefore wanted to make sure she had enough money in case of an emergency.

By the time they left the store, the stagecoach was pulling up to the office.

"Perfect timing," Ellen said with a smile. "Now, we just have a few more hours on the road."

Kate sighed at the thought. The train hadn't been extremely comfortable, but at least they had been able to stand up and move around. The stagecoach would have no such amenities.

"You ladies have your tickets?" the driver of the stagecoach asked as they approached.

"Yes sir," Ellen said and handed over her ticket. Kate followed suit.

"Alright," he said after looking them over. "Do you have any other baggage?"

"Yes, those trunks." Ellen pointed to the baggage sitting against the wall of the stagecoach office.

The driver nodded. "That's fine. I'll load them up. My name is Mr. Cooper. I'm going to check and see if we have any more passengers or a shotgun messenger. We don't often run without one."

"Does that mean we could be stuck here?" Kate asked as Thomas stepped into the stagecoach office. She had a little extra money, but she hadn't planned on having to stay at many inns along the way.

"I don't know, but I'm sure they'll work it out." Ellen tried to sound brave, but Kate didn't miss the uncertainty in her voice or the look of concern that crossed her face.

The driver re-emerged from the office with one stern woman and one mousy man following him. The man was continually pushing spectacles up the bridge of his nose. Kate hoped he wasn't their shotgun messenger as she wasn't sure he could hit the broad side of a barn.

"Are we not still missing one person?" Kate asked.

"No, it turns out we won't have a shotgun messenger on this trip as we aren't carrying a strongbox."

Kate wasn't sure whether that made her feel better or worse. With no strongbox, hopefully they wouldn't be a target for robbers, but the extra protection of the shotgun rider would have been nice.

"Alright everyone, I'll load up this last baggage, and we'll get on our way."

"Norman, help him out, why don't you?" the stern-faced woman said to the mousy man.

"It looks like he has it, love, and besides my back, you know?" He pushed the spectacles up again as he spoke.

The woman rolled her eyes. "Well, then help me inside."

"Yes, love," the man said. He opened the coach

door and held out his hand for the woman to help her up. Then he scrambled up behind her.

Ellen raised her eyebrows at Kate, who was forced to cover her mouth to keep from giggling.

"All ready, ladies?" Mr. Cooper asked as he approached them.

"Yes, thank you," Ellen said as she took his hand and climbed in the stagecoach. Kate followed suit and then the door closed behind her.

The interior of the coach surprised Kate. It was covered in a dark plush fabric and could seat four people comfortably. The stern woman and Norman had taken the far seat, so Kate sat next to Ellen.

"This is not that ba—" Kate began, but her words were cut short when the coach lurched forward, and she was thrown back against the seat.

"You were saying?" Ellen asked, her lips pulling up into a grin.

Kate shook her head. "That should teach me to speak too soon."

"I abhor these contraptions," the woman said, "but they are slightly better than traveling by horseback."

"Thankfully, we don't have far to go, love," the man said. "We're going to Belleville to visit my sister," he added for Ellen and Kate.

"I don't see why she couldn't just come to us," the woman harrumphed.

Kate and Ellen shared another smirking glance, and then the ride evened out. Kate became accustomed to the rhythm of the swaying coach. Though occasionally bumpy, the ride itself wasn't much worse than the train; however, the plume of dirt that resided out their window made it nearly impossible to see the passing scenery.

"While the accommodations are not that bad," Kate said, "I cannot imagine making the entire trip from Boston this way."

Ellen smiled and nodded. "Yes, it was quite a long trip to be sure. I much prefer the train where at least there is a privy and a place to clean up."

"I much prefer not to take such trips at all," the woman said.

The conversation halted after that, and Kate's mind turned to her future. She wasn't sure how much time had passed when the coach stopped suddenly.

Kate looked to Ellen. "Are we there already? That seemed awfully fast."

Ellen's eyes were wide as she shook her head and placed a finger to her lips in a shushing motion.

There was a commotion outside, and then the door of the coach opened. Ellen and the stern woman gasped as it was not the friendly face of their driver. The face of the man was covered by a red cloth. Only his eyes were visible, and they were a clear blue and as cold as ice.

"Hey, boss, we got a group of women in here," the man said.

"I am not a woman," Norman began, but his wife elbowed him, and he shut his mouth. Not in time though as he drew attention from the robber at the door.

"Correction, three women and one man."

"Bring em out, and make sure they grab all of their things," a voice hollered back.

"You heard the boss," the masked man said. "Grab yer things and git on out."

Kate wanted to refuse, but the gun the man brandished as he motioned them to get out kept her mouth shut.

Grabbing her bag, she stood and stepped down from the coach. Kate bit her lips together as she spied the driver face down in the dirt. She thought she could just barely make out the rise and fall of his chest. Kate hoped he was just unconscious and had not sustained a more serious injury.

"Don't worry, he'll be fine as long as he stays down."

As Kate looked up at the man on the horse who had spoken, he pulled his black hat even lower on his eyes. A similar cloth covered his face, and the only defining characteristic Kate could identify was the sling over his right shoulder. He appeared to have been injured recently.

Ellen climbed down beside Kate, and the two women clasped hands. The stern woman and Norman followed Ellen and stood on the other side of the door.

"Those sacks all you have?" the man on horseback asked as he gestured at the traveling bags clutched in their hands.

Kate knew he could see their trunks from his vantage point on the steed and guessed he was testing them.

"We each have a trunk," she said, pulling her shoulders back to present a brave front.

"You're a smart girl," the man said, and though Kate couldn't see his face, she would have sworn he was smiling.

"Mine holds mainly my clothes," she said. "Nothing of value."

"I didn't ask you what they held, girl." The man's voice had turned into a snarl. "Whether there is value in them or not is for us to determine."

Their trunks thudded to the ground followed by a third masked robber. The woman moaned as one trunk popped open and spilled its contents across the ground. Norman shushed her and pulled her closer to his side.

"Relieve them of their bags," the man on horse-back ordered, and the first man snatched their satchels from their hands. He loaded up the saddle-bags on one horse. "Get those other trunks open," the leader said to the third man, "and let's see what's in there."

The man on the ground obeyed and rifled through the couple's trunk that had opened on impact. He held up a wad of money before shoving it in a pouch and turning to Ellen's trunk. Dresses and jewelry went flying out of her trunk as he opened the lid and knocked it over.

The robber snatched up her jewelry, shoving it in a pouch and flung the rest of the clothes to the side. Kate felt Ellen stiffen beside her, and a glance out of the corner of her eye showed the older woman biting her lip.

Kate's trunk fared no better fate. He flipped the lid open, and Kate cringed when he grabbed her mother's brooch and shoved it into the pouch. She watched, helpless, as her other jewelry was added to his stash, but she could hold her tongue no longer when he held up her wedding dress.

"Please," Kate said. "Please let me keep my dress. I'm betrothed and supposed to be meeting my husband in Lisbon. Please do not make me get married in this." Kate motioned at the traveling dress she wore.

The man on horseback walked his horse over until he was directly in front of Kate. "Married, huh?"

She tried to keep her eyes on his to pretend she wasn't afraid of him, but his harsh gaze penetrated her thin wall of bravery, and she dropped her eyes. They landed on his left hand which was holding the reins of his horse. A white scar in the shape of a crescent moon resided there.

"Well, I certainly wouldn't want you wearing rags to your wedding." The man laughed as he turned his horse away. "Let's ride, boys!"

The men on the ground mounted their steeds after grabbing the remaining jewelry and money from Kate's trunk and the couple's trunk.

As they rode out of sight, Kate hurried to the driver on the ground. There was a gash across his head, but it appeared shallow, more likely from the butt of the gun than anything else. With the tip of her skirt, she wiped the blood away.

"I think he'll be okay," she said turning to Ellen. Ellen; however, was curled into a ball. Her arms were wrapped around her knees, and she was rocking back and forth. As Kate hurried over, she noticed the other woman had fainted and Norman was fanning her face. Kate wrapped her arm around Ellen. "It will be alright. It was only things."

"It was everything I had," the older woman murmured.

"We'll figure something out," Kate said, although she also wondered how she was going to pay for any other incidentals.

The driver was still unconscious when the woman woke. Her stern words were gone, and she was content to let Norman stroke her hand. Kate picked up the contents of the trunks while they waited for the driver to stir.

The sun had shifted considerably in the sky when Mr. Cooper finally felt able to continue the journey. Though none of them felt comfortable continuing on, they feared for their safety even more if they stayed put. After reloading the coach, Thomas helped the four subdued passengers back inside.

"How far are we from Sage Creek?" Kate asked the driver before he closed the door.

"Another few hours. We're about an hour out of Belleville."

"Let's stop and talk to the sheriff there in case the robbers come after the town. Do you think they would telegraph Sage Creek and Lisbon and let them know of our delay?"

"Yes, ma'am," he nodded. "I'm sure they will." With that, he closed the door, and Kate settled back against the seat.

"How is it you appear so calm about all this?" Ellen asked as the coach lurched forward again.

Kate bit the inside of her lip as she thought about how to answer. "I wouldn't say that I'm calm. I'm as angry as a hornet and scared of how I'm going to make it with no money, but I guess the difference is that I know Jesus is looking out for me. Even when I'm worried, He has a plan, so I'm trying to leave it in His hands. It's not like worrying helps solve the problem anyway."

Ellen sat back and regarded Kate. "I've never been one much for religion, but I think I'd like to hear more about this Jesus of yours."

Kate glanced over at the other couple, but when they didn't protest, she smiled and told Ellen of Jesus' love.

CHAPTER SIX

J esse sighed as he led Molly towards the stagecoach platform. The sun was setting, and he wanted to be home in bed concocting scenarios of revenge, but the telegraph of a stagecoach being robbed had come in a few hours ago. Being the new deputy and the only one without family (nothing like rubbing salt in the wound), he'd been given the task of meeting the stagecoach and taking accounts from the passengers.

He stiffened as he saw three people on the platform. Was he late? No, as he grew closer, he recognized the tall physique of James and the smaller outlines of Pauline's parents. What were they doing here? It wasn't as if he were avoiding them, but they served as a reminder of Pauline's death.

"Go home, Jesse," James said. "We don't need you here."

Jesse matched James's cool tone. "I'm here on sheriff business, James. It's my understanding this stagecoach was robbed, and I am here to collect the details of the encounter in order to begin an investigation."

"Oh, now you care about the robbers," James said snidely. "Too bad you couldn't care a few days ago before Pauline was killed."

Jesse took a deep breath to remain calm. "What are you doing out this late? Is there something I can help with?"

"We're here for the stagecoach," James spat. "My grandmother is arriving today. Even though she's older and missed Pauline's funeral, she's making the trip over from the east coast."

The words stung Jesse, and he narrowed his eyes at the man who was almost his brother-in-law. He had loved Pauline, and yet James was acting as if it had been Jesse's bullet that had killed her. Even if Jesse had been deputized on the day of the robbery, there was no guarantee the result would have been any different. He opened his mouth to say as much, but the look of sadness on Pauline's parents' faces kept him from it. There was no need to deepen their pain to satisfy his ego.

Moments later the sound of the approaching stage drew Jesse's attention. He sat straighter in his saddle, keeping his eyes peeled for any shadiness, but he figured the robbers would not be stupid enough to rob the same stage twice as nothing would be left to steal.

The stagecoach came to a stop in front of the station, and the driver jumped down to open the door. A nasty bruise covered his forehead, but he appeared in decent shape otherwise.

Jesse noticed there was no shotgun messenger. He would have to remember to ask if they had started with one.

When the coach door opened, an older woman with grey hair stepped down first, followed by a younger woman with dark locks.

"Mother," Pauline's mother croaked out through tears as she ran into the older woman's arms.

"Where is your sheriff?" the younger woman asked, her eyes glancing around. When they landed on Jesse, his breath caught. They were the bluest eyes he had ever seen. "We need to discuss the robbery to which we were subjected."

"I am a deputy sheriff ma'am," Jesse said, removing his hat as he spoke. "I'm Deputy Jennings, and I'll be taking that account down for you."

"Good." The young woman nodded at him and turned to the driver. "Mr. Cooper, would you be opposed to a brief layover before we continue to Lisbon?"

"No, ma'am," the driver stated "I could use some rest too, and it's dangerous to travel at night. We should wait and head out in the morning."

For the first time since the woman stepped off the coach, she appeared flustered. "But I have no money and no place to stay overnight."

"You'll stay with us," the older woman said, reaching out a hand to the younger woman.

"Oh, Ellen, I could not impose," the younger began.

"Nonsense," Ellen responded. "You kept your head when the attack happened and calmed me afterwards. It is only one night, but I will not hear of you staying anywhere but with us. Right, Iris?"

"Sure, yes," Iris stammered. "If you helped my mother, then our house is open to you."

Jesse stifled his sigh of irritation. He wanted to finish his duty and return home. "How about the three of you come with me then? I'll take your statements, and you ladies can be on your way. Mr. Cooper, was it?" he asked, turning to the driver. "We'll get you set up with a room at the inn."

"I don't think I'll be of much help," Ellen said. "I

was too scared to take much notice. I just remember there were three men."

"I'm sure my statement will be enough," the younger woman said. "Why don't you spend some time with your family, Ellen, and I'll get this nice deputy to drop me off afterwards. That won't be a problem, will it?"

Though she formed the words as a question, the tone behind them was more of a command. Jesse opened his mouth to say no, but the woman batted her eyes at him and smiled ever so sweetly. Before he could utter the word, he found his head nodding against his will in response. "It will be no problem Miss..." he trailed off as he realized he hadn't heard her name as of yet.

"Whidby. Mary Katherine Whidby."

"James, be a good boy and grab our trunks, will you?" Ellen asked sweetly before turning her attention to Jesse. "You do know where to take her after she's done giving her account, don't you?"

"Mother," Iris hissed, glancing sharply at Jesse. "This is *Jesse Jennings*; the man Pauline was going to marry."

Ellen's eyes grew round, and her hand flew to her mouth. "Oh, dear, I am so sorry. I should have realized from the name. I guess I'm still flustered from the robbery."

"It's alright, ma'am," Jesse said, swallowing the knot of emotion trying to climb up his throat. "But to answer your question, I do know where to take Miss Whidby."

Ellen stared at him a moment longer, then nodded. "We'll see you soon, Kate," she said, turning her attention to the younger woman.

As Pauline's family loaded up their wagon, Jesse threw Molly's reins around a nearby post. "If you three will come with me, the sheriff's office is just up the way."

Though Jesse led the way, he noticed that Miss Whidby stayed almost even with him in stride. Who was this woman and where had she come from?

After unlocking the door, Jesse pointed to the two chairs in the room and grabbed some paper and a pencil from the desk. He leaned against the edge as he looked from the woman to the driver. "Let's start with you, Mr. Cooper. Can you tell me what you remember?"

The man nodded. "We were traveling the path to Belleville when I came across a fallen tree. When I slowed the coach down, a man came out from behind one of the trees with a gun pointed on me. Before I could reach for my gun, two more appeared on horses. I guess one of them hit me with his gun because the next thing I remember is waking up to Miss Whidby's face."

The man shot an admiring glance at the woman who smiled but didn't appear to reciprocate similar feelings.

"Did you not have a shotgun messenger?" Jesse asked.

"No, we weren't carrying a strongbox, so they sent us on without one. I don't know why they targeted us," Thomas answered.

Jesse shook his head, unsure himself. "Perhaps they were hoping for wealthy passengers or perhaps they were just desperate. How about you, Miss Whidby? What do you remember?"

The woman drew herself straighter in the chair. "The coach stopped, and we heard a commotion. One of the men opened the door and ordered us outside. He wore a red cloth over his face, so all I remember were his eyes. They were blue and cold. Once outside, we saw another man on horseback. He also wore a mask and his hat low, so I couldn't see any of his face, but his right shoulder was in a sling as if he'd been injured recently."

Jesse stopped scribbling and looked up at the woman. "Could it have been from a gunshot?"

Miss Whidby shook her head. "I can't say for sure. I

don't remember blood on his arm, but I suppose it could have been from a gunshot. Why do you ask?"

Jesse tapped the pencil against the pad of paper. Could it be the same band of robbers? "Nothing, keep going, please."

"A third man came around the side of the coach and the two on the ground took our bags, dumped our trunks, and stole our money and jewelry. Oddly, the man on horseback allowed me to keep my wedding dress."

"Wedding dress?" Jesse asked.

"Yes. I am supposed to be meeting my husband in Lisbon."

Jesse realized he was staring at her and forced his eyes back to the paper. "Alright, is there anything else you remember that you can tell me?"

Miss Whidby closed her eyes for a moment as if mentally recalling the incident. Then her lids snapped open. "Yes, there was one more thing. The man on horseback had a scar on his hand."

Jesse's throat went dry. "A scar did you say? What type of scar?"

Her brow furrowed. "A small white one. Like a moon sliver."

Rage boiled within Jesse and he nearly snapped the pencil in two. "Where were you when you were attacked?" he asked the driver.

"About an hour east of Belleville," the man said. "We dropped two passengers off there and spoke with their sheriff who told us the robbers had hit them too."

This band was getting more dangerous every day. Three attacks in less than three days? The sheriff might be content to sit and wait for them to come back, but Jesse was beginning to feel more strongly that they would have to go after the men to get them to stop.

"Thank you both for your accounts," Jesse said, placing the paper and pencil back on the desk. "Mr. Cooper, let's get you settled in the inn and then I'll take you to the Masterson's, Miss Whidby."

Jesse led the way out and locked the office behind him. "The inn is run by Clark and Martha Davis," Jesse said. "I think you will find them quite accommodating."

"As long as it's a place to sleep, I'll be fine," Mr. Cooper answered.

The inn door was closed when they arrived, but after a few hard raps at the door, a light shone out of the window. A short older woman with grey hair and kind eyes answered the door.

"Hi, Miss Martha," Jesse said. "I'm sorry to bother you so late, but Mr. Cooper here is a stagecoach driver. They were robbed earlier today. He has no money to pay you, but he needs a place to stay."

Martha nodded and ushered the driver inside. "Of

course I will find him a place to stay. Do you need a place too, Miss?" she asked, turning her attention to Miss Whidby.

"No, thank you. I'm staying with Mrs. Ellen Baker."

"She's staying with the Mastersons, Miss Martha," Jesse said, trying to squash the emotion threatening his voice. "But thank you."

Martha's eyes widened, and she nodded knowingly. "Alright. Well, you have a good night, Deputy."

Jesse nodded and tipped his hat her direction. "Well, Miss Whidby, I have no wagon. Will you be opposed to riding on my horse?"

"Of course not," the young woman said with narrowed eyes. "I am an accomplished rider."

"I meant no offense, ma'am," Jesse said. Though he would never say so out loud, he admired this woman's spunk. "I was more concerned with your comfort because of the forced proximity between us on horseback."

"Oh," Miss Whidby dropped her eyes. "Thank you for your concern, but as there is no other option, it will be fine."

When they reached Molly, Jesse helped Miss Whidby onto the saddle first before swinging up behind her. Though he tried to keep as much distance between them as possible, he couldn't help smelling the intoxicating sweet scent of lavender wafting his way.

She turned slightly in the saddle, so she could see him and asked, "Ellen's granddaughter was your fiancée?"

Jesse looked away as he nodded. "Her name was Pauline, and yes, she was."

The woman opened her mouth as if to ask another question, but his cold gaze must have changed her mind as she shut it and turned forward again.

The rest of the trip to the Masterson residence occurred in silence. He pulled Molly to a stop, dismounted, and reached a hand up to help Miss Whidby down.

When her feet hit the ground, she looked up at him and said, "I'm sorry about your fiancée. I hope you find the men who did this. Thank you for the ride."

Before he could respond, she turned on her heels and walked away. Jesse waited until she was safely in the residence before mounting Molly and steering his horse towards home. Her last statement rattled around in his head. Would he ever find Pauline's killers and be able to avenge her death?

CHAPTER SEVEN

Kate swallowed her fear as she hugged Ellen goodbye on the platform. Though she knew she needed to get to Lisbon, a large part of her was afraid to step in the coach. What if the robbers struck again? Or worse yet, what if an entirely different band of robbers struck?

"How far is it to Lisbon?" she asked Mr. Cooper as he loaded her now much lighter trunk.

"It's about an hour, Miss."

"It will be fine," Ellen said, reassuring her. "You've told Deputy Jennings the story."

Kate glanced over at the stony-faced man on horseback near the coach. Evidently, he would be escorting them out of town. "I'm not sure what good it did."

Ellen followed Kate's gaze. "I know he seems stoic now—and I never met him before—but I knew

Pauline, and she would not have settled for anything other than a great man."

"All set, Miss," Mr. Cooper said from the front of the coach.

"I guess that's my cue," Kate said with a sigh. She hugged Ellen again before climbing into the coach once more. The driver shut the door, and Kate waved out the window.

When the buildings faded away, and the sagebrush took over the view, Kate sat back and thought about her future. She found herself wondering what her husband would be like. Would he be tall with broad shoulders? Would he have a beard? Would he have kind brown eyes?

Roughly an hour later, the coach stopped, and the door opened.

"Welcome to Lisbon, ma'am," Mr. Cooper said, holding out his hand for her to step down.

Kate glanced around as she took the driver's hand. Lisbon didn't appear much different from Sage Creek. As the platform was empty, Kate wondered how she was supposed to get in touch with her future husband, Bill Easterly.

Before she had time to worry, a wagon pulled up, and a man who appeared about thirty climbed down. He had average brown hair and eyes which narrowed slightly at her before he pasted a smile on his face.

"You must be Miss Whidby. I'm so sorry I'm late. I'm Bill Easterly." He held out his gloved right hand to take hers though Kate noticed he grimaced slightly.

Kate wondered if he were not pleased with her appearance. She had tried to fix her curls and smooth the wrinkles from her dress the best she could. With a tight smile, she placed her hand in his and nodded. "I am Kate Whidby. It is nice to meet you, Mr. Easterly." She had hoped to feel some sort of attraction with this man, but there was nothing. Did this mean she was in store for a loveless marriage?

"Oh, please call me Bill. After all, we'll be getting married shortly, won't we?"

Something in the way he said the words in a lecherous tone sent a shiver down Kate's spine. What had she gotten herself into?

"Do you have much luggage?" he continued.

"Just this trunk," she said, pointing to the large chest Thomas had gotten down for her. "I would have had a little more, but we were robbed on the way here."

"Oh, that's awful. Were you harmed?"

He was saying the right words, but there was still something about him that bothered Kate.

"No, thank goodness. They took my jewelry, but I did manage to convince them to let me keep my wedding dress."

"Well, that is all that matters," he said as he began to move her trunk into his wagon. "We can always make more money." Though he tried to hide it, Kate heard a small grunt as he lifted her trunk, and noticed he wasn't lifting the right side as high as the left.

"Did you injure your shoulder?" Kate asked.

Bill turned toward her, a hardness in his eyes.

"You appear to be having some trouble lifting with your right side," she said, pointing.

His gaze softened, and he smiled. "Oh, yeah, I hurt my shoulder roping some cattle the other day. I reckon it's still a little sore. It's nothing to worry about though."

Kate nodded. "I'll pray for a speedy recovery for you."

"Well, that'd be mighty nice of you," he said. "You ready?" He held out his left hand to her this time.

Though some intuition told her she should not get in the wagon with him, she had no excuse and she had made a promise, but she would be vigilant and keep her eyes open until she said "I do."

When the wagon headed out of town, Kate turned to Bill. "Aren't we heading to the preacher?"

"I thought you might like to see the farm first and get changed there," Bill said, flashing her a smile.

"Oh, that's nice of you," Kate said. It would be nice

to see the place she would be calling home from now on.

"So, you said you were robbed," Bill said, glancing at her out of the corner of her eye. "Did you get a good look at them?"

Kate had no idea why, but her inclination was to withhold the truth from him. "No," she said, shaking her head and hoping her voice wouldn't give her away. "I was too scared to notice much, and they wore masks. I only know that there were three of them."

"Ah, well, that's too bad," he said. "That isn't much to give authorities."

"No, it isn't," Kate agreed. "I doubt I shall ever see my things again. Most of it doesn't matter to me, but I do wish they hadn't taken my mother's brooch."

"It was important to you?" he asked.

"It was one of the last things I had of my mother's. She died a few months ago."

"Oh, that's too bad, but such is the nature of life I suppose," Bill said.

"I suppose," Kate begrudged, slightly shocked at his blasé dismissal of her mother's death. She was not the best at directions, but she tried to memorize the way out to Bill's ranch in case she needed to find her way back to town on her own after they were married.

"Well, there it is," Bill lifted his arm slightly to point.

The landscape dipped and allowed Kate to see a small ranch house. A horse was corralled on one side, and on the other side, a small creek ran by the house. Though this part of Texas didn't have many trees, Bill seemed to have several on his land.

"It isn't much I know," Bill said, "but I'm planning to expand soon."

"I'm sure it's lovely," Kate said. This time the smile Bill flashed her was sincere, and Kate almost forgot her misgivings. Almost. He stopped the wagon in front of the house moments later and helped her down.

"Would you mind if we just got your dress from the trunk?" Bill asked. "My shoulder is aching a bit, and I'm not sure I could carry it inside at the moment."

"No, that's fine," Kate stated. "I can take out what I need." She walked around to the back of the wagon and opened her trunk. Kate moved the other dresses aside until she found her mother's wedding dress at the bottom. It was of a cream silk, which had recently become popular when her mother married, and though it had a round skirt, rather than the now fashionable bustle and fish tail, Kate had always loved it. The neckline scooped just low enough to show off her collar bones and tiny rosettes lined the neck and sleeves.

Kate removed the dress—careful not to pull too hard—and then grabbed the matching gloves. The shoes didn't match exactly, but as Kate's feet were two sizes larger than her mother's feet had been, she had needed to supply her own shoes. She also grabbed her coat. Though it wasn't cold enough to need it, she still didn't want her groom to see her in her wedding dress before the ceremony, and as they had to drive back to town, that would be nearly impossible unless she were covered up.

"Alright, I'm ready," she said.

"Wonderful. Follow me, and I'll show you your room," Bill said, leading the way into the house.

The front door opened into a small main room. Kate imagined it could look a little homier with a handmade quilt. The kitchen was to the left, which appeared to have an older stove. Perhaps they could purchase some new cookware and utensils. There was a door at the back of the main room, which Kate assumed led to his quarters. Bill opened the door and held it open for her. It held a single bed and a small chest for her to put her clothes in.

"I'll leave you to get changed, and I'll freshen up myself," he said. "I rescheduled the wedding for dusk today when I received word your stagecoach was delayed."

Kate nodded and waited for him to shut the door before collapsing on the bed. The quilt covering it was tattered and threadbare. Nothing about this room seemed to show he cared about his future bride, deepening Kate's apprehension. Perhaps her brother had been right. What had she been thinking marrying a complete stranger?

Kate sent up a prayer for wisdom as she changed out of her traveling dress and into her mother's wedding dress. The dress still fit as perfectly as it had a year ago when she had snuck into her mother's closet and tried it on but wearing it now didn't hold the joy she had always believed it would. Was that because she didn't want to be married? Or because she might be marrying the wrong man?

She sighed and pushed the thought from her mind as she pulled on the gloves and slipped her feet inside her shoes. Then she folded her traveling dress and draped the coat about her shoulders. There was no looking glass in this room, so Kate was unable to check her appearance, but she tucked her hair back into place as best she could and pinched her cheeks to add some color before exiting the room.

Bill was sitting in the main room as she entered. "My, my, aren't you a sight?" he whistled.

The words should have brought a smile to Kate's face, but instead they caused the hairs on her arms to stand on end.

"Time's a wasting," he said, standing. "Let's head back into town, so I can make you my wife."

Kate noticed he was still wearing gloves as he held

out his arm to her. Had he injured his hands or were they deformed in some way?

She took his arm and followed him out to the wagon where he again helped her get in before climbing up beside her. The ride back to town was quiet as Kate's mind was on her future, and she had no idea what Bill was thinking.

The church was a small clapboard building with a single steeple which housed a bell. Though probably a bright white at one time, the paint was now faded and peeling, giving the church a dilapidated appearance. Kate wondered if anyone had any pride for this church.

Bill helped her down and led her inside. Rows of wooden pews lined either side of the aisle, and a single reed organ sat at the front of the church under a stained-glass window.

"Welcome," a voice said from the front. "I'm Pastor Jacob." A short man clad all in black stepped out from behind the pulpit at the front.

"Pastor, it's Bill Easterly. I've come with Kate Whidby for you to marry us," Bill said. To Kate he whispered, "Pastor Jacob has trouble remembering things from time to time."

"Oh yes, Bill," the preacher said. "I've been expecting you. Do you have the rings?"

"I do," Bill stated, patting his pocket.

"Wonderful," Pastor Jacob said. "If you are both ready, please remove your coats and gloves."

Kate removed her coat and gloves and laid them on the pew in the first row. Bill hesitated but removed his gloves as well.

"Please join hands," Pastor Jacob instructed, waving his hands in a motion to get them to step closer together.

After another small hesitation, Bill held out his hands to Kate. It was only a momentary flash as he quickly turned them palm up, but it was long enough for her to see the white puckered skin on his left hand. Her eyes widened slightly, and she forced herself to remain calm. What nightmare was she living in? This man wasn't just creepy; he was the robber. There was no way she could go through with this marriage, but how was she going to get away without arousing his suspicion?

"Do you have any guests?" Pastor Jacob asked, moving from side to side and scanning the church.

"No, it's just us," Bill said. "Can we get on with the ceremony?"

"I suppose, but it will change my wording. It's hard to say dearly beloved when there is no one out there."

Perhaps this was her chance. "I'm sorry," Kate said. "This was my mother's dress, and I think my corset is too tight. Is there a place where I might loosen it? I'm feeling rather faint."

"Are you alright?" Bill asked.

"I just need a moment. I'm sure I'll be fine," Kate said. "I just need to let the corset out a bit. My mother was a little smaller I guess."

"You can use my study just through that door," Pastor Jacob pointed to a doorway behind him.

Kate couldn't tell if there was an outside door attached to the room Pastor Jacob had pointed to, but she had no other choice. "I'll be right back," she said, smiling sweetly at Bill and hoping she looked convincing.

Kate hurried to the room, frowning slightly at the thought of leaving her coat, but there was no way she could grab it. The room held a small desk, and even more importantly, it had another doorway. As Kate put her hand on the handle, she prayed it led outside.

The light had receded while she'd been inside, and the air had cooled, but Kate didn't care. There was enough light from the moon to light her path. She took off running to the right. As she rounded the church, she saw a horse tied up to a nearby post. While Kate didn't believe in stealing, this might be her only chance to escape.

With one swift motion, she untied the reins and swung herself up onto the saddle. The wedding dress groaned in agony as it stretched in unexpected ways, and Kate found her airways slightly constricted. She dug her heels into the horse, urging it into a run.

She was almost past the last building when the shot rang out. It wasn't near her, but she could hear yelling behind her. Kate hunkered as low as she could on the horse and rode on, praying Bill would not find a horse or get his own unhooked from the wagon in time.

CHAPTER EIGHT

J esse had just finished feeding the livestock when a movement in the nearby brush caught his eye. Dropping his hand to the hilt of the revolver on his side, Jesse approached the brush.

He expected a wild animal or perhaps an escaped calf, but he was unprepared for the tattered and dirty creature he found instead. "Miss Whidby?"

Her dark hair was a tangled, matted mess with stray grass and weeds sticking out of it. Her dress, once probably clean and beautiful, was now covered in dirt and ripped in several places. Scratches lined her arms and face, their angry red marks standing in steep contrast to her alabaster skin.

"Bill?" she asked in a soft, confused voice as her eyes fluttered open for just a moment.

"No, it's Jesse. Jesse Jennings or Deputy Jennings." When she didn't respond, Jesse leaned down and picked her up. Her head flopped against his shoulder, and even in her current disheveled state, he could still smell a soft flowery scent.

After a quick glance around to make sure no one was lying in ambush, Jesse hurried toward his house, barely feeling the weight of the woman in his arms. He kicked open the door, crossed to his bedroom, and laid her down on the bed.

Unsure where to begin, Jesse grabbed a rag and dipped it in the washbasin. He wished he had someone he could send to fetch Doc Moore, but there was no one close. He would have to do what he could to patch her up and then load her up in his wagon when he was sure she could make the trip.

He brought the wet cloth back to the bed and touched a red mark on her cheek. It elicited a slight moan, but her eyes remained closed. What had happened to her? And who was Bill?

One at a time, he cleaned out the scratches and wiped the dirt off her face and arms. After three washings of the rag, he had cleaned off all the dirt and scratches he could see. With nothing else to do except wait for her to wake up, he covered her with a blanket, shut and locked the front door, and stretched out on the floor beside her.

The sun had set completely when he awoke later to the sound of Miss Whidby's voice. "God, please don't let him find me. Please Lord, protect me." She thrashed from side to side as if having a nightmare.

"Shh, Miss Whidby," he said, laying a hand on her head. "You're having a bad dream, that's all."

Her eyes snapped open. They were a deep blue like he imagined the color of the ocean at its deepest point might be. For a moment, they were dazed, glancing from left to right as she took in the surroundings. Then they landed on him and she scooted farther back on the bed.

"Deputy Jennings?" she asked. "How did I get here?"

"I found you in the brush by my barn. Can you tell me what happened?"

Her eyes closed a moment, and he thought she had fallen asleep again. "I was looking for you."

"For me? Why?"

Her eyes opened. "I found him. The robber."

"You found him?" Anger surged through Jesse. Had he been the one to injure Miss Whidby as well? Jesse wanted to tear out of the house and hunt the man down, but he needed a name, a description, something. "Who is he?" Jesse asked, but Miss Whidby had passed out again.

Jesse growled in frustration and fought the urge to

shake her. Whatever she had gone through must have been terrible, and she needed her rest, but there would be no more rest for him. Not until she awoke again and could tell him what happened.

KATE STIRRED as the first rays of morning filtered in through the windows.

"Where... Where am I?" Kate asked as she struggled to sit up. Her head pounded, and the room tilted in an unusual manner.

"Don't move too fast," a male voice said.

Kate looked to the voice, surprised to see Deputy Jennings's face looking back at her. She pulled the blanket up to her chin and shied away from him.

He held out his hand, and reluctantly Kate took it, allowing the deputy to help her sit up and lean against the headboard.

As soon as the deputy released her hand, he stepped back as if her very presence was fire. He crossed his arms and met her gaze. Kate wondered if there ever had been warmth in his brown eyes. "I found you on my property last night, and you were in pretty bad shape."

Kate closed her eyes and shook her head slowly. "I didn't know where you lived. I was just trying to get to

Sage Creek to find you because you are the only lawman I know."

"Yes, you said as much last night. You said you found him." A light seemed to enter him as he spoke of the robber.

"Yeah, I found him or rather he found me," Kate said with a snort. "I almost married him. His name is Bill Easterly. At least that's the name he gave me. He's a rancher in Lisbon."

"He lives that close?"

Kate blinked at the anger oozing from Deputy Jennings voice. "He took me to his house. I could probably find it again."

His eyes snapped up to meet hers, and a fire blazed in them before he sighed. "No, we need to get you to Doc Moore first. What happened out there anyway?"

Kate bit the inside of her lip as the hazy images came back to her. "I ran from the church as soon as I knew it was him. He wore gloves all day, but he took them off for the ceremony, and I saw the scar. There was a horse outside. I'm ashamed to say I stole it."

"I think the owner would understand," Deputy Jennings broke in.

"It still wasn't right," Kate said with a sigh. "I don't even know who to repay, nor do I have any money to do it. Anyway, before I was out of town, he must have realized I ran away. Shots were fired at me. I don't know if he fired them as I didn't look back, but I hadn't gotten far when I heard horses catching up to me. Knowing he had the upper hand with having knowledge of the land, I dismounted as soon as I saw some tall brush and sent the horse loose."

"But all the scratches and cuts," he began.

Kate rolled her eyes. "I got lost a few times, had to climb a few fences, and as I hadn't brought water with me, I am pretty sure I ended up dehydrated. I am honestly surprised I got as close as I did."

"Just another reason we should have Doc Moore check you out. Do you feel up to travel?"

Kate performed a mental check of her body. She ached all over and felt a little dizzy, but she attributed that to lack of food. "Yes, I think I'm alright. Could we possibly eat before we go?" she asked, placing her hand on her stomach. "I can't remember my last solid meal."

"I'm not much of a cook," Deputy Jennings said, holding out a hand to help her up. "But I'll try to throw some breakfast together."

Kate took his hand and stood, but she had moved too quickly, and the room began to sway. Her knees buckled, but the deputy's strong arms caught her, and she fell against his chest. She looked up into his eyes, and a flicker of warmth stirred in their chocolatey depths.

"Here, I got you," he said, averting his gaze and leading her out of the bedroom and to the kitchen. He helped her into a chair at the table before turning toward the stove.

For the first time since she met him, Kate caught a glimpse of what he must have been like before his fiancée's death. His stiff demeanor softened as he pulled out a skillet and set in on the stove top. After lighting the stove, he cracked a few eggs into the skillet and added a few slices of bread. Moments later, he was scraping half of the contents of the skillet onto a plate and heading back her direction.

"It isn't much, Miss Whidby," he said, handing her the plate and a fork, "but I wasn't expecting company."

"Please call me Kate," she said as she took the plate. "I feel like now that you've seen me at my worst, we should at least be on a first name basis."

The deputy ducked his head but nodded. "Then you should call me Jesse. Deputy Jennings is too formal anyway."

"Thank you, Jesse." She took a bite of the eggs and tried not to make a face. Kate had cooked often with her mother and knew something wasn't right with the eggs. Her hunger, however, kept her shoveling the food in.

Jesse filled his own plate and sat across from her. As he took his first bite, Kate chuckled as his face scrunched in disgust as well. His brown eyes met hers, and he smirked. "I'm sorry. I am not the best cook. I always went to Pauline's parents for dinner."

"What happened to her?" Kate asked, hoping she wasn't crossing the line.

Jesse dropped his eyes to his plate and pushed the eggs around. After a deep breath, he met her gaze. "She was an innocent casualty in a bank robbery. By the same men who robbed your coach."

Her eyes grew wide as her mouth formed a small O shape. "I'm so sorry. No wonder you want to find him so badly."

"I promised to avenge her," Jesse said.

Kate nodded. She could understand that. "Why didn't they kill us, I wonder?"

"Probably because you complied with their demands. There was another deputy in the bank the day Pauline was shot, and my guess is he tried to stop them. Pauline was just an unintended casualty."

"Perhaps it is none of my business, but it seems you really loved her."

"I did."

"Then why did her family appear so distant towards you?"

"Her brother blames me. They asked me to become a deputy when the robberies first started, but I was working on our homestead. I only took on the badge after she was killed, and I think her brother thinks I could have stopped it."

Kate wished she knew the right words to help or that wouldn't be too personal.

When they had both cleaned their plate, Jesse took the dishes and put them in the sink to wash later. "Let's visit Doc Moore to make sure you're alright."

"What will I do after?" Kate asked quietly. "I have no money, and what remains of my clothes are in Bill Easterly's wagon if he didn't get rid of them." She clasped her arms in front of her chest.

"Don't worry," he said, approaching her side. "We will figure something out. I'm sure the hotel will have a room you can stay in for a few days. As soon as we get you checked out, the sheriff and the other deputies and I will create a plan to round up Bill Easterly and return your things."

JESSE SAT outside the clinic while Doc Moore examined Kate. He shouldn't feel nervous. After all, he barely knew the woman, but she had been through so much already. The bravery she displayed was admirable.

The door opened, and Kate stepped out. "Thank you, Doctor," she said, before closing the door behind her.

Jesse stood, his hat in his hand. He wanted to ask her how it went, but that was far too personal.

"Just cuts and bruises," Kate said, reading his mind.

"That's wonderful news," Jesse said. "Shall we see about getting you a room at the inn?"

"Yes, thank you, and then I would really like to help you catch Mr. Easterly."

As Martha showed Kate her room, her husband, Clark, took Jesse aside. "We can only give her two days, Jesse. Money is tight, and we have to leave the room open for paying customers."

"She has nowhere else to go," Jesse said.

"I know," Clark said with a nod. "And that's why we're allowing two days, but then she'll have to find a job or a husband."

Jesse sighed. They both knew the only job for women in the West right now was at the saloons. "I understand. Thank you for the two days. We'll figure something else out for the rest."

Footsteps on the stairs halted any further conversing, and Jesse looked up to see Kate descending with Martha at her side. Kate's tattered dress was gone, and she was now wearing a dark blue cotton dress that, while a little big, accentuated her beautiful blue eyes.

"Does it look alright?" she asked, smoothing the skirt with a self-conscious gesture. "Martha was kind enough to loan it to me."

Jesse shook his head. "You look fine and definitely more suited to riding than with what you came in wearing."

"Right, yes," Kate said. "Well, shall we go get the sheriff and see about finding a robber?"

Jesse led the way out of the inn and back towards the sheriff's office. Sheriff Johnson looked up from the desk as they entered.

"Afternoon, Jesse. Who's this you got with you?"

"This is Kate Whidby. She was robbed outside Belleville by the same gang that robbed our bank and killed Pauline and Josiah."

"I'm sorry to hear that, ma'am," Sheriff Johnson said, nodding his head at Kate.

"She knows where one of them lives," Jesse finished.

The sheriff nearly knocked his chair over as he stood and slammed his palms on the desk. "Well, what are we waiting for? Let's go get the sucker."

"Can you draw us a map?" Jesse asked, turning to Kate.

"No, I'm coming with you."

"There's no way you are coming with us," Jesse

said. "It's too dangerous. What if Mr. Easterly is still there?"

"Give me a gun, then. I shot with my father and brother. I can protect myself. I'm no good at directions, but I could probably remember the route if I rode it again."

Jesse looked to the sheriff, expecting him to refuse, but the elder man shrugged his shoulders and said, "If she knows the way, then I guess she rides with us."

"Fine, but you don't approach the house with us. We have no idea what we might encounter, so you can take us as far as the homestead, but then you let us go in without you, understood?"

Kate opened her mouth as if to argue more, but then sighed and nodded.

CHAPTER NINE

"Which way now?" Jesse asked, his patience wearing thin.

Kate scrunched her face in thought. "Um, left, I think. Yes, left."

"Are you sure this time?" Once outside of Lisbon, Jesse had allowed Kate to ride alongside him to determine the direction, but so far, she'd made two wrong turns and cost them at least an hour.

"I'm doing my best," she excused. "I was only there once."

Jesse sighed and ran a hand across his chin. "You're right. I'm sorry. So, left?"

She looked around them again and then nodded with force. "Yes, left. I'm sure."

They moved further along the road until they crested a small hill. A house at the base came into view.

"This is it," Kate proclaimed triumphantly.

"That's far enough," Jesse said. "You sure this is the place?"

Kate frowned at him. "I'm sure."

"Okay, Jeb, you stay here with Miss Whidby. Jesse and I will go scout it out," Sheriff Johnson said.

Jeb nodded, and Jesse led the way down the hill, keeping his eyes open for any signs of the masked men. They tried to keep the horses quiet to aid in the surprise factor.

When they reached the front porch of the ranch house, Jesse pulled Molly up short. The cabin door was ajar. With one finger to his lips, he used the other hand to point the issue out to the sheriff who nodded.

The two men dismounted quietly and drew their guns. Sheriff Johnson led the way, pushing the door fully open with the muzzle of his gun.

As they stepped into the room, it was clear it had been torn apart. Chairs were upended, and clothes lay strewn about the room. The main room had a kitchen to the side, which was empty, but a doorway at the end of the room was closed. Again, Jesse took a cover position as Sheriff Johnson pushed open the door. A large bed filled most of the room. A silent, unmoving figure lay sprawled on the bed, a pool of red surrounding him.

"Kate said Bill Easterly had a scar on his hand," Jesse whispered. "We should see if it's him."

The sheriff nodded, and the two men stepped closer, still remaining alert for anyone else present. Jesse glanced down at the man on the bed. A gunshot to the chest had been his end, but neither of his hands displayed a scar. His ice blue eyes stared into nothingness.

"It's not him," Jesse said. "Let's get out of here." He took a step back and something crunched under his feet. Stooping down, he picked up the shattered pieces of what might have been a broach or a locket. He dropped the pieces in his pocket to show to Kate. Perhaps the item had belonged to either her or Ellen.

Jesse followed the sheriff out of the house and back up the hill where Kate and Jeb were waiting.

"It wasn't Easterly," Jesse said. "No scar. This man had blue eyes, and it looked like there had been a fight."

Kate nodded. "One of the other robbers had blue eyes, the one who opened the coach door. Did you find any of my things?"

"We need to speak with their sheriff to search the house more, but I did find this. Does it mean anything to you?"

He dropped the pieces in Kate's hand. For a moment, her brow furrowed as she tried to make sense of the shattered item, and then tears fell freely from her eyes. "This was mine. My mother's broach. The last thing I had of hers."

Jesse's heart ached at her tears. He knew that emotion all too well. The only thing he had left of Pauline was a handkerchief she had once given him. When he wanted a piece of her near, Jesse would pull it to his face, inhaling her fresh scent of sage which still lingered on it.

Shaking Jesse from his memories of Pauline, Sheriff Johnson said, "Jesse, why don't you take her back to Sage Creek. Jeb and I will work with the men here to see if we can't find any more items," the sheriff suggested.

Jesse nodded and looked to Kate. "Can you ride?"

"I'll be fine," she sniffed. "Let's go."

JESSE COULDN'T STOP THINKING about Kate after he dropped her off at the inn. Clark Davis had said they could grant her two nights, which meant she only had more night after tonight. Unless Sheriff Johnson found some of her jewelry or money, she would have no way to continue paying for her room nor would she have the money to return home. And he needed her to stay. She was the one person who could identify Bill Easterly and help him avenge Pauline's death.

But to stay, she would need to marry or find employment, and Jesse knew the only place hiring women right now was the saloon. His Christian duty and desire for justice conflicted with his heart, and he pointed Molly toward the cemetery. Though she wouldn't be able to answer, he needed to discuss this idea with the one woman it would matter to.

KATE MADE sure Jesse had left before she slipped out of the inn. With no money, her option now was to find employment. She set out first for what she thought was the school house. After all, she had taught back in Boston. It couldn't be too different here.

The school day was just ending when Kate arrived at the building. A flurry of children raced past her and out of the door. When she was sure they were all gone, Kate stepped into the doorway. A young brunette woman was gathering papers at the desk up front.

"Excuse me," Kate said.

The woman stopped her shuffling and turned to look at her. "Can I help you?"

"Yes, my name is Kate Whidby. I'm new in town,

and I was wondering if there might be a job here at the school?"

The woman shook her head. "I'm sorry, Miss Whidby. We don't have enough children to need two teachers."

"Oh, I understand," Kate said, swallowing her disappointment. "Thank you anyway." She turned to leave and then paused. "Do you know of any place in town that is hiring?"

"Just the saloon," the woman said with a sad smile.

"Right, thank you."

A feeling of despair crept in on Kate as she left the school building, but she decided to try the other establishments anyway. Unfortunately, she received a similar response in the general store, the cafe, and the post office.

Shoulders slumped, Kate returned to the inn. Perhaps the Davises would have some work she could do.

"Why the long face, Miss Kate?" Martha asked as Kate entered the parlor.

"I was out looking for a job," Kate said, her eyes downcast. "But no one is hiring." She glanced up. "I don't suppose you need help here at the inn?"

Martha's brow creased. "No, I'm sorry, dear, we don't. It's been a tough winter for everyone around here."

"I understand," Kate said with a tight smile. "I'll figure something out, I'm sure."

"Why don't you sit down, and I'll get you some tea?" Martha asked, pointing to an empty table.

"KATE? ARE YOU ALRIGHT?"

Glancing up from where she was having evening tea, Kate watched as Ellen hurried across the room towards her. She set her tea cup on the table and stood to greet her friend. "Ellen? What are you doing here?"

"James told me he saw you riding out of town with the sheriff and the deputies this morning. What happened? I thought you were getting married."

Kate shook her head and motioned for Ellen to join her at the table. "Would you believe that the man I was supposed to marry is the same man that robbed us?"

"What?" Ellen covered her mouth as she sank into the chair.

"Yes, I suppose I have rotten luck," Kate said and paused to take a sip of her tea. "Something seemed off about him when he picked me up, but when I saw the scar on his hand I ran. I went looking for Deputy Jennings, got disoriented along the way, and he found me near his home. We rode out there this morning, but Mr. Easterly was gone. I don't know what I'm going to do now, Ellen. Even if they find my clothes, the money and jewelry will be long gone. I have no money to pay for my room here, and I knocked on all the establishment doors this afternoon. The only place in need of work is the saloon which I can't do. I came out here to get married, so I wouldn't be a burden to my brother, and I couldn't even do that right."

Ellen leaned back and regarded Kate. "Perhaps you could stay with us."

Kate shook her head. "I couldn't do that. Your family doesn't know me and they're in mourning for their daughter. It would be too big of an imposition. Maybe I could telegraph my brother and ask for money. I know Abigail might object, and I hate the idea of being an even bigger burden to him than I already am, but I don't see as I have any other option."

"Well, there is one other option," Ellen said.

"What's that?" Kate inquired.

"You could still get married."

"Didn't you hear what I said?" Kate asked, confused. "The man I was going to marry is a thief and a murderer."

"I didn't mean him," Ellen said, waving her hand. "But this is the West. In case you haven't noticed, there are far more men than women. Maybe you could find another man looking for a bride. It would be worth at least checking the papers before you head back."

Kate bit her lip. Could she do it? What if she chose another outlaw like Bill? Surely the odds of that happening again would be unlikely, but with her luck?? Of course, it might be better than admitting to her brother she was wrong. She could just imagine his reproachful look when he learned she had lost all the money.

"You're right," Kate said with a sigh. "I guess there's no harm in at least looking."

JESSE LEFT the cemetery with a sense of purpose. It wasn't how he had planned his life to go, but he felt at peace with his decision.

The lanterns at the inn were still lit when Jesse arrived. After a deep exhale, he dismounted Molly, tied her to the post, and knocked on the inn door.

"Deputy Jennings?" Martha asked as she opened the door. "Is everything alright?"

"Yes ma'am," he said, removing his hat. "I was just wondering if I could speak with Miss Whidby for a minute?"

"Let me tell her you're here. Why don't you go have a seat in the parlor?" Martha pointed to her right, and Jesse walked that direction as she turned to go up the stairs.

No one else was in the parlor, so Jesse chose a straight-backed chair near the entrance and sat down. His hands curled and released the brim of his hat as he waited for Kate to arrive.

"Jesse? To what do I owe this visit?" Kate stood in the doorway, her dark hair down and framing her face.

Jesse stood and cleared his throat. "I've come with a proposition for you, Kate. I know we don't know each other well, but I also know you have no money to keep paying your room here or to purchase a ticket home."

"I was planning to wire my brother and ask for money to make the trip home which wasn't a perfect scenario as the whole reason for me coming out here was not to burden him, but Ellen gave me the idea of looking for another man in search of a wife..."

"The thing is..." Jesse interrupted, holding up his hand to stop her rambling. "I need you to stay here since you're the only one who knows what Bill Easterly looks like. Which brings me to my solution; I could use some help at the homestead. You tasted my cooking." A nervous laugh bubbled out of his throat, and he cleared it again. "I guess what I'm saying is I have a proposition that would help us both out."

He paused and glanced at Kate for a reaction, but her face was stoic. He got the feeling she didn't like being interrupted. "We could get married," he said quickly before he lost his nerve. "That way you'd have a home, and I could protect you in case Easterly showed up again, and if we ever find him, you would be able to identify him."

Jesse forced his mouth shut to stop the flow of words. He needed to give her time to think and process. He continued curling and uncurling his hat brim as he waited for her to answer.

Kate tilted her head and stared at him. "I knew coming out here I wasn't marrying for love, but I hoped I would at least find a decent man and a nice home. While my time here hasn't gone as I'd hoped, I would prefer an alternative to returning home and burdening my brother again. Since I am limited in my options, and it seems this arrangement would benefit the both of us, then yes, Jesse, I accept your proposal."

"Okay," Jesse said with a nod. "I'll speak with Pastor Lewis and set it up for tomorrow afternoon." He glanced at her attire, which was a simple cream top and navy-blue skirt. "Do you need time to get a dress for the wedding?"

Kate shook her head. "The sheriff dropped off my trunk of clothes a few hours ago. I can find something which will work for the occasion." She gave him a tentative smile. "I appreciate all of you going after him and returning my possessions, even if it wasn't the sole reason."

"You're welcome," Jesse said as he stood and replaced his hat. "Have a good evening, Miss Whidby, and I'll see you tomorrow." As he left, Jesse wondered what he had gotten himself into. Kate Whidby was nothing like his docile Pauline had been.

CHAPTER TEN

K ate stood in front of the mirror inspecting her appearance. It didn't matter whether she turned left or right, the pale blue dress felt far too plain to be getting married in. If only her mother's wedding dress hadn't been torn and dirtied.

A knock sounded at the door and Martha stuck her head in. "Good morning. Mr. Davis told me the good news, and I thought maybe I had something that might help. Can I come in?"

"Certainly," Kate said. "I don't look like much of a bride anyway."

"Maybe I can help with that," Martha said as she entered the room and shut the door behind her. "Mr. Davis and I never had a daughter, but I kept this anyway." She held out a long cream dress with a lace neckline and ruffled sleeves. "I think I was a little bigger than you, but we could tie the sash tighter and add a few carefully hidden pins."

Kate's eyes flooded with emotion. "Why are you doing this for me? You barely know me."

Martha smiled. "That may be, but we know Jesse. He has always treated people fairly and done what he can to help, just like he's doing now. You both have had a rough patch starting out, but maybe you can find a greener pasture together. Besides, here in Sage Creek we take care of our own, and since you're about to be one of us, I can't have you getting married in a blue dress, pretty as it is."

"Thank you," Kate said, wiping a tear from the corner of her eye. "I hope you'll come to the ceremony. It would mean a lot to me."

This time it was Martha's turn to sniff. "Of course Mr. Davis and I will be there, and I have a feeling we'll see a lot more of each other. Now, let's get you into this dress."

JESSE STOOD at the front of the chapel rocking back and forth on his heels. When he'd told Clark about his decision to marry Kate, the man had offered to bring her to the church at the appointed time and serve as a witness. Yet, the church bell had just finished ringing two o'clock and there was still no sign of them.

Jeb and Sheriff Johnson looked at him with raised eyebrows from their position in the front row. Clearly, they thought he had been stood up. Jesse swallowed his apprehension and shook his head. Maybe this had been a big mistake.

"I'm sure they'll be here shortly," Pastor Lewis said as Jesse looked toward the front doors once more.

A few moments later, the doors opened, and Martha hurried in, waving her hands. "I'm sorry we're late. We had to do a quick change."

Kate stepped in next, and Jesse's breath caught in his throat. Her dark hair was pulled back with combs except for a few tendrils that framed her face. The cream dress she was wearing showed off her slim waist and made her eyes appear even more blue. There was no denying she was a beautiful woman.

A NERVOUS SMILE pulled on Kate's lips as she stepped into the small chapel. A blond man with small spectacles in a black suit and white collar stood at the front near Jesse. In his hands was an open book. Kate assumed he must be the pastor.

Next to him, Jesse stood in a similar black suit only

without the white collar. Instead, he wore a high collared white shirt with a black tie. His dark hair was combed, and his face appeared even more chiseled without his hat.

As she walked up the aisle, she realized the sheriff and Jeb were sitting in the front row as guests for Jesse. She was glad Mr. Davis and Martha had come with her.

"I hope you don't mind me saying so, miss, but you look beautiful," Mr. Davis whispered and patted her hand in a fatherly gesture before joining Martha in the front row.

A light pink covered her cheeks as she stopped beside Jesse.

"Hello ma'am, I'm Pastor Lewis," the pastor said softly. He had a kind voice and seemed much more with it than the last pastor who had almost married her. "What's your full name?"

"Mary Katherine Whidby," Kate said. "But everyone just calls me Kate."

"That's fine," the man said with a smile. His gaze shifted from her to the people in the pews as he began. "Dear friends, we are gathered here today to join Deputy Jesse Jennings and Mary Katherine Whidby in holy matrimony. Jesse, do you take this woman to be your lawfully wedded wife? To protect until death do you part?"

"I do," Jesse said.

The pastor turned to Kate. "And do you Kate take this man to be your lawfully wedded husband? To cherish until death do you part?"

"I do," Kate said.

"Do you have rings, Jesse?" Pastor Lewis asked.

Kate was surprised when Jesse dug in his coat pocket and pulled out two gold bands. She'd had no idea he had purchased wedding rings.

"Very well, place the ring on Kate's finger and repeat after me."

Jesse clasped her hand and put the ring on her finger as he spoke, "With this ring, I thee wed."

A tingle ran up Kate's arm and she glanced up to see if Jesse had felt it, but he was focused on placing the other ring in her palm.

"Kate, if you'll put the ring on Jesse's hand and repeat after me," Pastor Lewis said.

Kate fumbled with the ring but managed to secure it on Jesse's hand and repeat the words.

"Then by the power vested to me by God and the great state of Texas, I now pronounce you husband and wife."

As THEY EXITED the hotel after gathering up Kate's

things, Jesse turned to her and said, "I know this isn't what we both imagined for our futures, but we can make the best of this situation if we both agree to try. I promise I will be a loyal and kind husband."

A smile formed on her lips as she nodded. "I want to make this work as well. I will do my best to be the kind of wife you need."

"Alright then," he said and held out a hand to help her into the wagon.

She settled on the seat, and he climbed up beside her and pointed the wagon toward his homestead.

Kate wasn't sure what she had expected in marrying a near stranger, but as she stepped down from Jesse's wagon, the enormity of her decision landed on her shoulders. She would now be sharing a house with a man she barely knew, and they hadn't discussed intimacy. Kate assumed as this was more a marriage of convenience that they would wait until they knew each other better, but she realized they should have discussed it.

"I'd give you the tour," he said with a small smile, "but you've been here before."

It did Kate's heart good to see him nervous as well. "That's alright. You could give me the tour anyway."

Jesse smiled and opened the door. "Well then, come inside and while you get situated, I'll come back out and get your trunk."

Kate inspected the house from a woman's standpoint as she entered. It was nothing grand, but it did have a homier feel than Bill Easterly's place had. The kitchen was clean and everything appeared to have a set place. The main room housed a few chairs and a small couch. Beside the bedroom was another door which Jesse pushed open to display a wash basin and a freestanding tub.

"You have a tub in a separate room?" Kate asked with surprise. Even in Boston, only the rich had a separate room for tubs.

"I saved up for the tub and added the room as I was building. It was going to be my wedding present to Pauline," Jesse said with a sad smile.

"Oh, I'm sorry." Kate felt awful for reminding him once again of Pauline but was glad to know he had cared enough about his future bride to do something nice for her. Another stark difference from Bill Easterly.

"It's fine." Jesse cleared his throat and continued the tour. "You can sleep in the bedroom, of course, and I'll take the couch in the main room," Jesse said. "I'll grab your trunk and be right back."

Well, at least that answered the question of whether he expected intimacy or not. Kate wandered into the bedroom while Jesse returned to the wagon. A wrought iron bed covered in a quilt sat squarely in the middle. She wondered briefly if Pauline had made the quilt.

There was a dresser with a mirror and a small table beside the bed, and on top of the table, Kate was delighted to find a Bible. If Jesse were a believer, then perhaps this could be a happy marriage after all.

She had just picked up the book when he re-entered with her trunk. "I'm sorry," she said, dropping it back on the table.

"Don't be," he said. He set her trunk on the floor and crossed to her. "Are you a believer?"

"I am," she said. "I was worried I might not marry a Christian man, but I guess God was watching out for me after all."

"Would you like to go to church with me on Sunday, then?" Jesse asked.

"Yes, I would love that."

As they shared a smile, Kate began to feel that maybe everything would be alright after all.

CHAPTER ELEVEN

Kate woke early the next morning. Though it had been nice sleeping in a real bed, it still wasn't a bed she was used to.

She pulled a dress on and opened the bedroom door quietly but was surprised to see Jesse already awake and reading at the table. "I'm sorry. I thought I would be up before you," she said, stepping into the kitchen area.

"I'm always up early to read," Jesse said with a smile. "I feel it's my best time with the Lord." He gestured at his mug. "I made some coffee; do you drink it?"

Kate shook her head. "No, I'm afraid I never developed a taste. Do you have any tea?"

"Fraid not, but as it's Saturday, we can go into town

and get some. The sheriff gave me a few days off to help you get situated."

"That would be wonderful, thank you. Have you eaten?" Kate asked, feeling like she should be doing something. "I could make breakfast."

"Breakfast would be nice," Jesse said.

After a few moments of fiddling with the stove, she managed to light the burner and set a skillet on to warm. In the icebox, she found eggs and bacon and added them to the skillet. Soon the sound of sizzling bacon filled the room. Kate found a bit of bread left and added it to the skillet to warm.

When everything was ready, she loaded up two plates and brought one to Jesse and set the other down for herself. Before he picked up his fork, he closed his eyes and Kate followed suit.

"Lord, thank you for this food you have provided for us. Help keep us safe and help us to keep our focus on you. Amen."

"Amen," Kate echoed. She watched with bated breath while Jesse took a bite of his food, hoping it would meet his standard.

His eyebrows arched up as he glanced up at her. "This is really good, Kate. Much better than the fare I was making myself."

"I wasn't going to say anything," Kate said with a smile, "but you could use some cooking lessons."

"I'm sorry you had to wake up to your first day in Sage Creek to my cooking. I'm glad you're taking over that chore, as I might very well end up poisoning the both of us," he said with a chuckle as he returned her smile.

It was amazing how much it changed his face. The hard lines disappeared, and tiny crinkles appeared at the corner of his eyes. Kate wasn't sure how, but she was determined to bring that smile around more often.

JESSE GLANCED at Kate as they pulled into town. While she wasn't Pauline, she had a charm about her, and her cooking was definitely an improvement on his own.

"I need to stop in and talk to Sheriff Johnson for a bit. Are you good to get the food items you need on your own?" Jesse asked as he pulled up in front of the general store.

"I think I can manage," Kate replied.

Jesse helped her down from the wagon and placed a few bills in her palm. "Get whatever you need, and I'll be back in a minute to help you load it up." Jesse watched her walk into the general store and then turned toward the sheriff's office.

"I see you couldn't wait to replace Pauline," James

said as he stepped out of the saloon and into Jesse's path. The smell of alcohol filled the surrounding air.

"It's not like that, James. Kate is the only person who knows what the man who killed Pauline looks like, and she needed a home. I had one. It's as simple as that."

"You can tell yourself that all you want," James said, poking a finger in Jesse's chest, "but it looks like you've replaced her to everyone else."

"James, go home and sleep it off," Jesse said, stepping out of the way. "We can talk more when you have a clearer head."

"This isn't finished, Jesse Jennings," James roared, but he lumbered the opposite direction, using the sides of the buildings to keep himself upright.

Jesse sighed as he continued to the sheriff's office. James was another problem he would have to deal with soon, but his most pressing concern was still Bill Easterly.

The sheriff was seated at his desk, scanning papers.

"Any word on Easterly, sheriff?" Jesse asked as he sat across from the sheriff.

"He hasn't returned to his house, but a few nearby towns have telegraphed they have seen him, so apparently he's still in the area. Unfortunately, they are out of my jurisdiction, and we can't just go mounting up without an invitation."

"So, are we still just waiting and hoping he shows up again?" Jesse tried to contain the frustration in his voice.

"It's all we can do right now. I'm sorry."

Jesse sent up a silent prayer for patience before saying, "Understood, sheriff. I'll just be sure to keep my eyes open should the opportunity arise."

Kate was exiting the general store as he returned, her arms laden with packages.

"Here, let me help you with those," he said, relieving her of a few of the parcels. "Did you find everything you needed?"

"Yes, thank you," Kate said, but her eyes were cast down.

"What is it?" Jesse asked as he placed the parcels in the wagon.

"Nothing, let's just go," Kate said.

Jesse wanted to press the issue, but he didn't want to cause a scene. As the wagon pulled out of town though, he turned to her. "Please tell me what happened."

Kate sniffed. "There was a woman in the store who heard we got married. She told me I had no respect for Pauline marrying you so quickly after her death. Will they all treat me like this? What good is staying if I'm to be an outcast?"

"No, not everyone will treat you like that," Jesse

said, gritting his teeth. He wanted to turn the wagon around and find out who the woman was and talk some sense into her. "Most people in Sage Creek are kind, decent folks, but you have to remember that Pauline was born here, so some folks have known her a very long time. I know they will come around once they get to know you."

As Kate flashed him a small smile, Jesse felt a sliver of the emotional wall he had built around his heart chip away. He hadn't known her long, but he had been telling the truth. There was something about Kate that was endearing, and he knew the town would accept her if they would give her a chance.

AFTER THE INCIDENT at the general store, Kate didn't much feel like attending church the following day, but she refused to stay home and become the subject of idle gossip. Besides, she had been missing the closeness to God she felt while at church and wanted to rekindle that emotion.

She pulled on her nicest dress and grabbed a hat for her hair. A glance in the mirror showed her dark hair hanging in uniformed ringed curls around her face. Kate pinched her cheeks and pursed her lips to give them some color and then exited the bedroom.

Jesse sat waiting for her in the main room, wearing a similar suit to the one he had gotten married in. "Are you ready?" he asked, glancing up from his Bible as she walked in.

"As I'll ever be, I guess," Kate said with a false bravado.

Several other wagons were in the church yard when they arrived, and they joined the throng of people walking in on foot. Kate squared her shoulders as they entered the small chapel, and she prepared for the onslaught of conspiratorial whispers and aside glances she expected. What she hadn't been prepared for was Ellen calling her name and hurrying her direction.

"So, it is true," the elder woman said as she took in Jesse standing by Kate's side. "I wasn't sure if I should believe James as he was drunker than a skunk when he told me."

"Are you mad?" Kate asked, biting her lip. "I wanted to tell you, but it happened kind of suddenly. Jesse showed up after you left the hotel that night, and I don't know," she shrugged, "it just made sense."

"Mad? Of course I'm not mad, silly girl," she said loudly, her voice carrying across the room. "In fact," she lowered her voice and leaned in, "I rather feel like it makes us almost family. You marry the man who was almost my grandson-in-law? I'm glad you did it."

"You might be the only one," Kate said, glancing around. "I don't think everyone else is so happy."

"Nonsense. When they get to know you like I do, they will love you. Now, let's go get a seat and let them gossip behind us."

Kate laughed at the elder woman's nonchalance and felt her anxiety slide away. Ellen was the one person she had hoped not to anger in her decision, and if she could accept Kate and Jesse, then Kate would be fine.

WHEN THEY RETURNED FROM CHURCH, Kate asked Jesse for a pencil and some paper. It was high time she wrote her brother and let him know she was alright.

Paper in hand, Kate closed the bedroom door behind her and sat down at the dresser to write.

Dear Robert,

I am sorry it has taken me so long to correspond. My trip has been adventurous to say the least. I met a wonderful woman on the trip. She reminds me very much of Mother as she's young at heart. Our stagecoach was robbed. Don't worry, I am alright, though the money I brought with me is gone. God has provided me with a kind, Christian man for a husband though and we are getting along fine. I hope all is well with you, and I look forward to hearing from you soon.

Kate

Kate reread the letter. Well, it wasn't the entire truth, but that was a little much to write in one letter. Perhaps she could tell the story in little bits. Satisfied, she folded the letter and sealed it in an envelope. She would mail it out tomorrow.

CHAPTER TWELVE

J esse woke to the early morning sun's rays coming in the window. He had overslept. With a start, he jumped up from the couch and reached for his trousers. He had just gotten them up when the bedroom door opened, and Kate walked in.

"Oh, I'm sorry," she said, holding a hand to her eyes. A soft pink blush flooded her cheeks.

"It's okay," Jesse said, tucking his shirt in. "I'm dressed now. You can open your eyes."

"I suppose I should get used to seeing you like that," Kate said, but he noticed her eyes remained focused in the opposite direction.

He bit back a smile as he answered, "Most days I'll be up before you will. It's not often I sleep in, but I can also take to changing in the washroom if it makes you feel more comfortable."

"Oh, that is not necessary," Kate said as she entered the kitchen. "After all, this is your house."

"It's our house now," Jesse said as he filled the kettle with water to make the coffee. It was the one cooking area Kate was still challenged in as she didn't drink it, so he often made it himself. In all other areas of the kitchen, though, Kate was extraordinary. She was not only a great cook, but an excellent baker. In fact, her cooking was so good that Jesse had been forced to let his belt out a notch.

Another flood of pink filled her cheeks at his statement, and she turned quickly to the stove. She opened the fire box, but the matches kept going out before she got the wood lit. Had he made her nervous?

"Here, let me help." Jesse reached for the match in her hand but ended up grabbing her hand instead. Her eyes turned up to his, and Jesse found himself falling in their blue depths. He shook his head to clear the image of her lips that had flooded his brain and forced himself to focus on igniting the firebox for her.

"Thank you," she said and held his eyes a moment longer before reaching for the skillet.

"You're welcome," Jesse said and finished his task of making the coffee. As it boiled, he thought about the last few nights with Kate. At first, she had just been a woman sharing his house, but he had come to see she was courteous and kind. In the evenings, she would often darn his socks or knit while he read from the Bible. It was for all these reasons that he felt the need to do something special for her.

"Kate, would you like to go for a ride this afternoon?" he asked, after swallowing his mouthful of delicious pancake. "I'd like to show you the sage fields near here, and the weather is supposed to be warm."

"I would love that," Kate said, and her blue eyes sparkled. "It feels like I haven't been on a horse in forever, if you don't count the night I was fleeing for my life, that is."

"Then it's settled. I will saddle up the horses after I finish this wonderful meal, and we will go for a ride."

JESSE FOUND himself whistling as he saddled up the horses after breakfast. As he finished cinching the saddle on the mare, his whistling ceased, and he paused. He shouldn't feel happy, should he? Shouldn't he still be mourning Pauline's death? He had felt, at the gravesite when he talked to her, that Pauline would be alright with his decision to marry Kate, but would she want him to be happy with her? Confusion clouded his previous happy mood as he gathered the reins of both horses. With a sigh, he walked back toward the house where Kate was waiting.

Her dark hair flowed freely today and lay in waves against her shoulders, and he wondered briefly what it would feel like between his fingers.

"Which one is mine?" she asked, breaking up his daydream. Her eyes held a mischievous gleam.

"This is Sadie," he said, holding out the mare's reins to her.

"Hello, Sadie," she said as she placed her hand on the horse's nose and rubbed. "She's beautiful, Jesse."

"Thank you," he said, "Shall we get going then?"

She nodded, and he helped her into the saddle before returning to mount Molly.

"So, are these fields how the town got its name?" Kate asked as he led the way to the lavender colored fields that lay on the outer edge of town.

"That's actually a funny story," Jesse said. "Evidently, there was a family feud when the town was first being founded. One half moved out near the sage fields and wanted to name the town Sagewood. The other half moved out toward the creek and wanted to name it Creekville. Eventually, they reunited and decided to combine names. Hence, Sage Creek."

"Well, I think it's a lovely name," Kate said with a

smile. "I've always loved sage. I think it's because purple is my favorite color."

"Then you are in for a treat," Jesse said.

A few minutes later, the land sloped down, and a sea of purple lay before them. Kate gasped beside him.

"I've never seen anything like it," she said in a voice filled with awe.

Jesse smiled and led the way down the slope. Huge purple sage bushes filled the area and looked like arcs of purple with only a thin row in between them. The sage brushed against their legs as they went down one of the rows. Near the far-left corner was a large weeping willow tree. Jesse led the way there, and they tied up the horses.

"So, tell me about your family," Jesse asked as he spread a quilt down for them to sit on.

Kate sat, curling her legs to the side. "What do you want to know?" she asked.

"Honestly?" Jesse asked with a smile. Kate nodded. "Well, I want to know what happened that made you want to be a mail order bride?" He hoped she wouldn't consider that too personal of a question.

Kate tilted her head and pursed her lips. "It wasn't in my grand plan if that's what you are wondering, though I'm not sure what was. I loved learning, and I loved riding, but the right man never came along. I received two proposals of marriage; one was from a lecherous older man and the other from a non-Christ-ian. I couldn't bring myself to marry either of them. Shortly after the last proposal, my parents got sick with Yellow Fever and I took care of them while my brother finished college. They never fully recovered, and they passed away.

"With my father being unable to work for many months, the house rent wasn't met, and I was forced to move out and rely on the mercy of my brother, Robert. It might not have been so bad, but Robert had just gotten married and his wife detested having to take me in. With the lack of any new proposals, I decided to try something different."

"I'm sorry you had to go through all of that," Jesse said tenderly.

She paused and traced a pattern on the quilt before meeting his gaze again. "Will you tell me something about you now?"

"I guess that's only fair," Jesse said, though he hoped she wouldn't ask about Pauline.

"How did you end up in Sage Creek?"

Internally, he sighed with relief at the topic of her question. "I was actually born in the East like you. We lived there until I was about fifteen when my little sister died. My father took it hard and decided to move us out West, but my mother had a weak immune system. She died a year later, and I couldn't forgive my father. I moved out here when I was old enough to make it on my own."

"Have you spoken to your father since?" Kate asked in a quiet voice.

"I tried to a few years ago when I accepted Christ, wanting to make amends, but he had passed away a few years after I left. So, I've been on my own ever since."

Silence fell between the two until Kate said softly, "I guess we have each other now."

Jesse looked at her and smiled. "Yes, I guess we do. Would you like to go have lunch at the cafe today?"

"I'd like that," Kate said.

They stayed a little longer watching the sage sway slightly in the breeze before packing up and heading back to town.

After tying up the horses outside, they stepped into the Sage Creek Cafe and chose an empty table near the front.

They had just finished enjoying a meal of roast and cornbread when James's voice thundered behind them. "When will you get it in your head that we don't want you and your fake replacement bride around here?"

Kate's eyes widened, and her hand flew to her face as everyone in the cafe turned and stared at them.

"James, you are out of line," Jesse said, standing. "Kate has done nothing to you. She didn't even know

Pauline. I know you miss your sister. I do too, but you have to let this go."

"You can't tell me what to do." James was trying to be forceful, but the slurring of his words diminished his effectiveness.

"Actually, James, this badge here says that I'm the law and I can tell you what to do. Now, you're making a scene, and I'm asking you nicely to leave this establishment. Go home and sleep off whatever liquor you drank."

James's answer was to swing a fist wildly at Jesse. It missed its target and sent James off balance. His good leg couldn't carry all the weight, and he fell to the floor with a great thud. A series of gasps and exclamations echoed throughout the room.

"I'm going to see if I can find someone to take him home," Jesse said to Kate. "Will you wait here for me?"

Kate nodded, her eyes still wide.

Jesse helped James stand and ushered him out the door. "You aren't under arrest, James, but we're going to find someone to take you home," Jesse said as they walked out the door.

KATE WATCHED Jesse and James exit before she allowed the tears that had been building up in her eyes to fall.

She had finally been starting to feel like she was being accepted, but James's outburst shattered that image. Would she always have to be reminded she wasn't Jesse's first choice and was only his wife because Pauline had been killed?

"Don't listen to him," a voice to her right said.

Kate looked up to see a young waitress, looking down at her. The woman appeared about Kate's age, maybe a year or two younger, with dark hair and brown eyes.

"I'm Sarah Miller, and I work here at the café. I want you to know, we don't all feel like James does," she affirmed. "We miss Pauline, but from what Miss Ellen says, you're a wonderful person. If she vouches for you, it's only a matter of time before everyone sees what she does. I, for one, am glad you're here. It's nice to have another woman close to my age around, and I hope we can become friends."

"Thank you," Kate said, sniffing, "but I don't know if I can keep dealing with so much hatred."

"Yes, you can. James doesn't hate you. He's just grieving. What you need is to get more involved with the rest of the women in town. There's a social this Sunday after church. There'll be dancing and food and a recipe swap. If you come, I promise you'll find more people who feel like I do."

Kate wiped her eyes and smiled at the girl. "Thank

you. I accept your offer. I haven't met many people my own age, and I could certainly use the socialization."

Sarah patted her arm. "I've got to get back to work, but I look forward to talking with you more on Sunday."

CHAPTER THIRTEEN

Kate was excited when Sunday morning dawned. Though the social wasn't until after church, she had gotten everything ready the night before.

She pulled back the sides of her raven locks and secured them with combs, letting the rest of the hair flow freely around her shoulder. As this was her first social and after church, she had picked one of her nicer dresses, unsure of what to expect. When she was satisfied with her appearance, she glided into the main room.

Jesse looked up from the table where he was reading. "You look lovely, Kate," he said.

"I'm not overdressed?" she asked, twirling around for him.

"Maybe a little," he laughed, "but I don't think anyone will mind. Are you ready then?"

"Wait, one more thing." Kate hurried back into the bedroom and grabbed the recipe cards she had written out the night before for the recipe swap. It had been a painstaking and tiring process, and she'd had to stop often to shake out her cramped hand, but she had a stack of cards to swap for today. And she was excited to obtain some new recipes to try for Jesse.

With the papers in hand, she hurried back to the kitchen and grabbed the bread she had baked the previous day to share. "Now, I'm ready."

Jesse smiled and shut his book. "Come on then."

Though Kate normally loved church, she found it hard to sit through the service today. She was too excited to socialize with other young women her age, and she couldn't remember the last time she had danced.

Jesse turned to her as she fidgeted in the seat yet again. "The time doesn't go any faster the more you move," he whispered with a smile.

"I know. I'm sorry." Kate forced her hands to remain still in her lap for the remainder of the service.

When the final hymn was sung, she stood and

glanced eagerly towards the door, but a parade of people standing and chatting blocked the path to the exit. She was forced to swallow her impatience once more, post a smile on her face, and exchange pleasantries as the line slowly filed out of the church.

As the social was being held in the barn not far from the church and the weather was fair, they decided to walk, but Kate had to stop at the wagon to grab her bread and cards. Then they joined the rest of the people heading toward the barn. It appeared nearly everyone in Sage Creek came out for socials.

As they neared the entrance of the barn, Sarah waved from the doorway. "Kate," she said, hurrying over. "I am so glad you were able to make it."

"Me too," Kate said, smoothing her skirt with her free hand. "Though I'm a little nervous."

"There's no need to be. I promise this will be a friendly crowd, right Deputy?" Sarah asked, turning to Jesse.

"Yes ma'am," Jesse nodded. "Jeb will be checking in to make sure no one from the saloon wanders over after too many drinks."

Kate knew he was referring to James, who still seemed to be harboring a grudge against them both, but she didn't mind. Today, she was going to enjoy herself and not worry about James.

"Come on," Sarah said, tugging on Kate's arm.

Kate looked to Jesse, not sure what the protocol was.

"Go on," he said. "I'm going to do a quick walk around, and then I'll come find you."

After saying goodbye to Jesse, she followed Sarah into the barn. There was a small band playing the banjo and harmonica on one side of the barn for the couples that wanted to dance. At the far back was a table filled with food, and on the left, tables had been set up for the recipe swap and general mingling.

"Let's drop your bread off first and then grab a table," Sarah said, pulling Kate toward the back.

Kate laughed and followed Sarah's lead. For the first time in a long time, she felt lighthearted and carefree.

"Kate? Oh, I'm so glad you're here."

Kate turned to see Ellen coming toward them. "I wanted to apologize for James's behavior," she said, pulling Kate in for a hug. "When I heard what happened, I wanted to come and see you right away, but Iris has been sick."

"Oh, no, is she alright?" Kate asked.

"Yes, I think it's just exhaustion. She had been going nonstop to try to forget Pauline's death, but when I finally made her take a break, her body told her she needed more rest. I think it's partly why James has been drinking more lately. I'm afraid he thinks he's going to lose her too. I was hoping maybe you could pray for all of us. I've been doing it, but I'm so new to this that I'm not sure I'm doing it right."

"There's no right way to do it, but I'd be happy to, Ellen," Kate said. "Why don't you join Sarah and I for the recipe swap?"

Ellen glanced over at the other young girl. "No," she said. "I may be young at heart, but I think you need to be with women closer to your own age today. You girls have fun."

As Ellen walked away, Sarah pulled Kate over to the recipe swap area. "What did you bring?" she asked Kate.

"My mother's sourdough bread recipe," Kate said. "What did you bring?"

"A bread pudding recipe. I'm a much better baker than a cook which is odd since my folks own the cafe right?"

"No, I get that," Kate said. "My mother loved to sew, but she always dragged me to fabric stores with her. I hated sewing growing up. I am still not very good at it."

"But perhaps there's hope for me yet?" Sarah asked with a smile.

"Wait until you get married and have to be the cook. You'll learn real fast," Kate said with a chuckle.

The girls laid out their cards and then meandered

through the other tables, picking up cards for other mouthwatering recipes. Kate was pleased to find a few for main dishes as that was her weakness.

When they had gathered all the cards, they walked to the back table to try some of the tantalizing food. The display was eclectic with everything from chili to savory desserts. After filling a plate with some, they headed back toward the table, but Jesse intercepted them on the way.

"Perhaps Miss Miller can put your plate on the table for you as I'd like to dance with you," Jesse said, taking her plate and passing it to Sarah before propelling Kate to the dance floor.

"I can't remember the last time I danced," Kate began as Jesse moved her in a circle around the floor.

"I've never been very good," he said. "I hope I don't step on your toes."

"Well, even if you do, I think I could forgive you." Kate smiled up at him, enjoying the feel of his hand on her waist.

He said nothing, but as he returned her smile, Kate realized again how handsome he was. His nose wasn't exactly straight, but it complemented his strong jaw, and the warmth of his brown eyes softened the chiseled lines of his face.

As the slower beat of the first song ended and a faster one began, Jesse didn't let go of her but upped his tempo in turning her around the floor. He managed to only step on her toes once, but the look of intense concentration on his face tickled Kate so much that when the song ended, she found herself flushed and out of breath.

"Can we go outside for a minute of fresh air?" she asked.

Jesse nodded, and taking her arm, led her outside. The cooler air tamed the heat on her face and neck but did nothing for her parched throat. She cleared her throat, trying to ease the dryness that had taken root.

"Would you like some punch?" Jesse asked. "I would be happy to fetch you some."

"I would love that," Kate said. "I'll just be out here catching my breath."

As Jesse ducked back into the barn, Kate leaned against the old rail fence and closed her eyes. Her trip out West may not have started on the best foot, but she was certainly content with it today.

"You're a hard woman to find, Miss Whidby."

Kate's eyes snapped open at the dark, throaty voice that did not belong to her husband. Brown eyes met her gaze, but they were not the warm chocolate pools of Jesse's eyes. They were instead a harsh and unforgiving brown like the desert, and they looked at her over the barrel of a Colt revolver.

"My name isn't Whidby any longer," Kate said with a forced bravado. "It's Jennings."

"You think just because you married someone else you don't belong to me?" he laughed a cold, cruel sound that turned Kate's blood cold. "I paid for you to come here. I own you, and if you were stupid enough to marry someone else, then it will be easy enough to end his life and free you up again."

"Why do you want a wife anyway?" Kate retorted. "Did you expect I would start robbing with you or just turn a blind eye?"

"I expected you would do what I told you to do. You would cook my meals and clean my house and fulfill your wifely duties."

Kate shivered at the insinuation in his words. "You were stupid to come here. The sheriff and his men are looking for you."

"That may be, but that's why I chose now. I know everyone is inside at the festivities and there's no one patrolling today. Once I found you, it was just a matter of playing the waiting game. Now let's get moving."

Kate glanced toward the door for Jesse. What was taking him so long?

"I don't think she'll be going anywhere with you."

Kate sighed with relief at the sound of Jesse's voice, but it was short lived as Bill grabbed her arm and swung her against his chest as he turned around. She saw just a flicker of fear enter Jesse's eyes as she was made into a human shield.

"I think I'll be making the rules here," Bill snarled. "Besides, why does she even matter to you? I'm sure you only married her for convenience."

The smell radiating off Bill was sour and acrid, and Kate could feel his sweat from the arm wrapped around her.

"She does matter to me," Jesse said, his eyes meeting Kate's for a minute, "but more than that, you are also responsible for killing my fiancée and one of our deputies, so I am taking you in one way or another."

"Your fiancée? Oh, you mean the pretty blond who was shot when we robbed the bank? I can see why you'd be upset about that. She looked like she could keep a man happy."

Kate saw the veins in Jesse's neck tighten. She had no idea how good of a shot he was or how accurate Bill was, but she also wasn't sure how much longer Jesse could keep his composure with Bill speaking ill of Pauline. What she was sure of though was that due to her height, Bill's left arm wasn't able to reach across her chest enough to pin her right arm down, and she knew that his right arm had recently been injured. She just hoped Jesse would remember and understand her gesture.

When Kate was sure she had Jesse's eye, she flicked her eyes to the right in hopes he would remember Bill's injury. Then, closing her eyes and praying, she flung her right arm up as hard and as fast as she could. When it collided with Bill's right arm, she felt his left loosen and she dropped to the ground as one, then two gunshots went off.

Kate clasped her hands over her ears as they began to ring from the noise and looked around. Bill lay on the ground behind her, a pool of red spreading across his chest. His eyes still held a look of shock. She turned to where Jesse should be standing, but he was also on the ground.

"Jesse," she cried as she scrambled over to him. There was no blood on his chest, but she ran her hands over it all the same feeling frantically for a wound.

When her hands reached his face, his eyes opened. "Kate Whidby. That was either the dumbest thing or the bravest thing I've ever seen anyone do."

Kate smacked his chest, causing him to grunt. "Don't scare me like that. I thought you were dead, and my name is Kate Jennings."

"So, it is," he said with a smile.

Moments later they were surrounded by half the town and peppered with questions. Jeb and Cody helped remove the body of Bill Easterly as Sheriff Johnson helped Jesse up.

"You're bleeding," Kate gasped as she saw a red spot form in his sleeve.

"It's just a scratch," Jesse said. "You knocked his arm wide enough that his bullet just grazed me."

"We still better get it looked at," Sheriff Johnson said. "Everyone else can return to the social. The danger here is taken care of."

The crowd stepped back a few feet, but no one seemed eager to hurry back into the barn. People murmured amongst each other, trying to guess what had happened.

Doc Moore emerged from the crowd and led the way to his office. "Let's get that shirt off, Jesse, and take a look at that arm," he said as Jesse sat on the cot in the room.

Jesse had barely felt the graze, but as he lifted his arm to begin unbuttoning his shirt, an achy sensation descended on his arm. He tried not to grimace, but from the look on Kate's face as she watched, he hadn't been entirely successful. After another few jabs of pain, he managed to get his sleeve off.

While Doc Moore examined and cleaned the wound, Jesse's eyes drifted to Kate. She was so unlike Pauline, not only from her dark hair and blue eyes but to her personality. He couldn't imagine Pauline doing what Kate had done. Though he still loved Pauline—he figured he always would—he realized there was room in his heart to care for Kate as well. Maybe in not quite the same way, but Jesse thought their marriage could not only be successful but happy and fulfilling as well.

"You're very lucky," Doc Moore said as he wound the bandage around Jesse's arm. "The bullet missed your bone, but it did go through a little of your muscle. It will heal, but you may be sore for a month or so, and you should take it easy with this arm for at least that long."

"Yes, sir," Jesse nodded. He was glad to see the fear had gone from Kate's eyes at the doctor's proclamation of his health.

"I know you said you weren't injured, Kate," Doc Moore said, turning to her, "but I'd like to check your ears and do a quick examination to be sure."

As Kate nodded, Jesse, and the sheriff exited the office to give her some privacy.

"I'm sure Ellen will let him know, but I suppose I better find James and tell him we got Pauline's killer," the sheriff said.

"Actually, sir, would it be alright if I did that?" Jesse

asked. "We've had our share of disagreements, but I'd really like to be the one to give him the news."

The sheriff nodded, and a moment later, the door opened, and Kate exited. "I'll walk with you," Sheriff Johnson said, "as I'm sure he's in the saloon and Miss Kate doesn't need to be in there."

"Where are we going?" Kate asked, looking from one man to the other.

"To tell James we got Easterly," Jesse said.

The sheriff led the way, and while he went inside, Jesse and Kate waited outside the saloon. A moment later, they heard James's deep voice protesting, "I don't want to see Jesse."

"You will for this," came the sheriff's voice.

Jesse's sullen face appeared in the doorway, followed by Sheriff Johnson's.

"James, I know you blame me for Pauline's death," Jesse began, "but I promised her I would find her killer. I wanted to let you know that we did. His name was Bill Easterly, and he came here tonight, but with Kate's help," he flashed her a smile, "we were able to outsmart him. He's dead, James. It's over."

James looked from Jesse to Kate to the sheriff. Though he had obviously been drinking, his face sobered. "He's dead? You really got him?"

Jesse nodded, surprised to see liquid forming in James's eyes.

"Good," James said, and walked back into the saloon.

Jesse watched him go and shook his head.

"Now, you two go home and get some rest," Sheriff Johnson said to Jesse and Kate, "but I want you both at the office tomorrow to give your account of what happened. I'll make sure James gets home and inform the Mastersons what happened. I hope it can give them some peace."

"Yes sir," Jesse said. As he turned to Kate, he held out his good hand. "I guess we better follow orders and get on home."

"There's no place I'd rather be," Kate said putting her hand in his.

EPILOGUE

"**T**ell me again why we're doing this," Jesse said as he buttoned his shirt.

"Because they're our friends, and they didn't get to come to our wedding. Well, except for Jeb and Sheriff Johnson and the Davises that is," Kate said. She tucked a stray strand of hair behind her ear and turned from the mirror. "Besides our last night of dancing was cut short. Now, we get another chance."

Jesse grabbed her hand and pulled her up to his chest. "You know we could dance right here." He spun her in a circle around the bedroom.

"Stop," Kate said with a laugh. "Come on now. Sarah will be hurt if we don't show up. She and Ellen planned the whole celebration."

"I know," Jesse groaned playfully. "That's what I'm worried about."

Kate batted his arm, which was now fully healed, and grabbed his hand, pulling him out of the door.

THE BARN HAD BEEN DECORATED with white flowers and lace. Lanterns created a romantic atmosphere as Kate and Jesse entered the wide doors.

"Congratulations," Sarah cried, running over to Kate and enveloping her in a hug.

"You do know we've been married for months now, right Miss Miller?" Jesse asked.

Sarah shot him a look. "Yes, but now the whole town supports your marriage. Look, even James showed up."

As if on cue, the large man limped over. His foot was nearly healed, but evidently the break had been bad enough that he would have a slight limp the rest of his life.

"I wanted to say I'm sorry, Jesse," James began, "and you too, Kate." He glanced at her under lowered lids. "I was wrong to blame you, and I'm glad you were able to get justice for Pauline."

"I am too," Jesse said, sticking out his hand. James looked at it for a moment before returning the shake with his own.

Kate smiled at the scene. God really could work miracles.

As more of the townsmen came up to speak to Jesse, Kate let Sarah lead her to the side where the women were congregated. Kate was surprised to see the girl who had shunned her in the store her first day in town standing in the middle of the women.

"I don't think we've officially met," the girl said, stepping forward. She didn't offer a hand though. They stayed behind her back. "I'm Rebecca, and Pauline was my best friend. I'm sorry for the way I treated you, and I wanted," she looked around her, "we wanted to tell you how brave we think you are. You've kind of become a role model." She brought her arms forward, revealing a wrapped package.

Kate took the package and looked around at all the women.

"Open it," they said.

Kate tore the paper back and lifted the lid. Inside was a beautiful quilt.

"We each brought a square of fabric from home and sewed it together," Sarah said. "It's a wedding quilt for your bed. Sorry we couldn't invite you this time, but we hope you'll join us for the next quilting bee."

Tears welled up in Kate's eyes as she regarded each of the women she now considered a friend. "Thank you," she said, her voice choked with emotion. "This means so much to me."

"Well, you mean a great deal to us," Ellen said, coming to her side. "See, I told you they'd love you when they got to know you," she whispered in Kate's ear.

Kate nodded, feeling happier than she could remember being in a long time.

A few minutes later, she was reunited with Jesse as Sarah brought out a large wedding cake. They cut the cake amid cheers from the crowd, and then Jesse grabbed her hand and led her to the dance floor.

"Alright, I have to admit," he said, "I do enjoy parties, especially when they give me an excuse to dance with you."

"Me too," she said, smiling up at him. "Oh, I forgot to tell you. I finally got a letter back from my brother."

"That's wonderful," he said as he twirled her around. "How is he doing?"

"Well," she said with a mischievous smile, "it turns out I'm going to be an aunt soon."

He stopped mid twirl and tightened his grip on her waist. "That is good news indeed, and it reminds me of something I'd like to ask you."

"What?" Kate asked with a tilt of her head.

"Well, with Easterly taken care of and things

calming down in town, I wanted to ask you what you thought of motherhood?"

"I think it's a very noble profession," Kate said, biting back her smile.

"Indeed it is," he said, "but I suppose my question was more would you like to be a mother?"

"I would like that very much, Deputy Jennings." This time she didn't bother to hold back the smile.

"As would I," he said. Their gazes locked for the briefest of moments and then Jesse leaned his head down to touch Kate's lips with his own.

The End!

IT'S NOT QUITE THE END!

Did you enjoy — Lawfully Matched? If you did, please leave a review. It really helps. http://books2read.com/LM

You won't want to miss the other ones in the series!
    Turn the page for a sneak peek!

14

AUTHOR'S NOTE

First off, let me say how glad I am that you read this book. Lawfully Matched was my first historical romance, and while it was fun, it was also a lot of work researching. However, I enjoyed it so much I did two more historicals. Then I got sucked back into contemporaries, but if you love historicals, you should send me an email. I have plans to return to Sage Creek.

And if you've enjoyed reading this author's note so far (and really, how could you not?) I am offering, for today only, a page where you can sign up for my weekly newsletter for the low, low price of absolutely nothing.

Included in this weekly newsletter are many wonderful things like pictures of my adorable children, chances to win awesome prizes, new releases and sales I might be holding, great books from other authors, and anything else that strikes my fancy and that I think you would enjoy.

Even better, I solemnly swear to only send out one newsletter a week (usually on Tuesday unless life gets in the way which with three kids it usually does). I will not spam you, sell your email address to solicitors or anyone else, or any of those other terrible things.

Join me here and receive a free novella as my thank-you gift for choosing to hang out with me. It's fun and entertaining. I promise.

Prayers and blessings,

Lorana

15

NOT READY TO SAY GOODBYE YET?

Kate and Jesse were such fun to write that I didn't want to let them go, so I put Emma and William in the same town.

Sage Creek is up and coming, and I have more stories for it, but let's take a look at Emma and William's story.

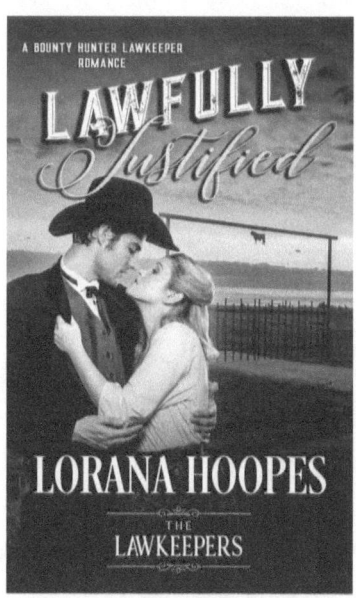

Lawfully Justified

HE's a bounty hunter who has given up on love...

William turned to bounty hunting after he lost his wife, but when he ends up injured in Sage Creek, he can't help noticing his attractive nurse maid.

She lost her husband but still wants a family...

Emma was happily married until her husband was killed on a mission. She wasn't looking for love again, but the handsome bounty hunter needs her.

The secret may tear them apart....

When William realizes his past is connected with Emma's he tries to run, but God has a different plan.

Read on for a taste of Lawfully Justified....

16

LAWFULLY JUSTIFIED PREVIEW

William "Wild Bill" Cook smoothed his black duster and stepped through the swinging batwing doors into the saloon. His eyes scanned the bustling, noisy room for the slim, bearded man whose face he had memorized from the Wanted Poster, but he didn't appear to be in the room. Of course, that meant nothing. Sometimes the men tried to disguise themselves or hide in low lit corners. Occasionally, he even found them upstairs with one of the saloon girls, if they had the money. Once he had even found a mark upstairs pretending to be a saloon girl. He hadn't been the brightest one, not realizing his full beard was a dead giveaway. It didn't matter. Wild Bill Cook always got his man.

He sidled up to the bar, pulled his black hat low on his eyes, and ordered a Whiskey. He wasn't a big drinker - his wife had hated the stuff - but he found one drink honed his senses and allowed him to survey the room without standing out too much. The last thing he needed was someone recognizing he didn't belong and warning Frank Monroe. The man was a cattle thief, and no man liked the prospect of jail time and most fought tooth and nail not to go.

When the drink slid his way, William picked it up, trying to ignore the cloudy film on it - Catherine would roll over in her grave if she saw him drinking from such a cup - and adjusted his position so that his back was to the bar.

A heated poker game was taking place at a table across the room, but a closer look ruled out any of those men. Another few men sat at a table closer to his position, tossing back beers, but they were all too large to be his mark. His eyes continued to scan left, but after coming up empty, he finished his drink and turned back to the bartender. Monroe must be hiding out upstairs then.

"Who do you have working tonight?" William asked the bartender. "It's been a long ride, and I'd like to unwind."

The long-haired bartender smiled at him, revealing a bottom row of crooked teeth. "What's your flavor?"

William shook his head as he spun the glass on the counter. "I'm not particular. What are my choices?"

The bartender scanned the room. "Looks like we have two blonds, Nellie and Lizzie, down here which means Minnie, my brunette is upstairs, engaged in other business."

"I guess I'll take a blond then," William said.

"Nellie," the bartender hollered across the noisy room. He cocked his head in a "come here" gesture, and a moment later, a plump blond appeared at William's side.

Her blond hair was pinned to one side and curled. Bright red lipstick covered her lips along with a dark rouge. A blood red dress trimmed in a black fringe hugged her frame a little too tightly, sending her extra flesh rolling over the top. William forced his eyes to remain on her face.

"You looking for a good time, honey?" she asked, laying a hand on his arm.

William resisted the urge to shake her hand off. She was his ticket upstairs, and he could swallow his revulsion a moment longer to apprehend his man.

"Sure am. Are you good at giving one?"

"I'm good at everything, honey." Her voice flowed like silk out of her mouth, but it had no effect on William. He hadn't been with a woman since the death of his wife, and he wouldn't until he married again. IF he married again.

"Lead the way then," he said, pushing the glass

back to the bartender and standing. Nellie headed for the back stairs, sashaying her ample hips as she walked. William kept his eyes peeled for Monroe as he followed her, just in case he had missed the man in his initial scan. It didn't happen often, but William stayed alive by always checking twice if the opportunity presented itself.

With each step, the wooden stairs groaned under his weight and William held tight to the railing as he climbed. The top of the stairs opened into a small hallway. Two doors were on the left and two were on the right, but all were closed. How was he going to determine which room Monroe was in?

"Do you girls all have a regular room?" William asked, hoping her answer would let him know which room Monroe was in.

"Sort of," Nellie said with a shrug, "but there are three other girls, so we have to share."

Not helpful. He'd have to be more direct. "Which one is Minnie's regular room?" William narrowed his eyes as he listened, but he heard no sound coming from any of the rooms.

Nellie's smile faded, and she crossed her arms. "Are you here for Minnie or for me?"

William scanned her face. While he didn't trust her - he trusted no one - he had little choice but to ask for her help if he wanted any chance of surprising Monroe.

"Honestly ma'am, I'm here for the man who is with Minnie. If you can point out her room, I'll pay you for your time."

Nellie's eyes widened and then she smiled. "Sure, her room is the second one on the left."

William tipped his hat and headed that direction. His right hand fell to the hilt of his revolver as his left turned the handle. Monroe and a brunette turned his direction as the door opened.

"Run, Frank," Nellie shouted from behind William.

A look of surprise followed by a flash of fear crossed Monroe's face before he rolled out of the bed and dove for cover. With a grumble, William whipped his gun out. He hated when things didn't go according to plan. "Frank Monroe, you're coming with me. You're wanted for stealing cattle."

The brunette pulled the sheet around her and let out a blood-curdling scream. The noise distracted William just enough that he didn't see Nellie run up behind him until it was too late. She rammed him with her shoulder, sending him into the door jamb.

A shot went off, followed by two more female screams. William thought at first that he had fired his gun when Nellie hit him, but then the searing pain just above his clavicle hit him. Monroe sat on the floor, his gun smoking in his hand. William tried to raise his arm to fire a shot, but it would no longer obey his command.

As soon as Monroe realized he had the upper hand, he scrambled up, but before he could make it very far, the thunder of footsteps reached the second floor.

"What's going on here?" the bartender demanded, splotches of red lighting up his face and emphasizing the scar that resided there.

"That's Frank Monroe," William said, gritting his teeth through the pain. "He's a wanted man, and I'm bringing him in. This one ought to be under arrest for abetting a felon." He pointed at Nellie with his left hand, trying to ward off the darkness that was creeping in on his vision.

"You can't arrest my girl," the bartender roared.

"Actually, we can," a male voice said from behind the bartender. Before the darkness won the battle, William noticed a star pinned to the man's chest. At least his man wouldn't get away.

Continue reading Lawfully Justified.

17

A FREE STORY FOR YOU

Enjoyed Lawfully Matched? Not ready to quit reading yet? If you sign up for my newsletter, you will receive Once Upon a Star, the love story of Blake and Audrey, two of my Star Lake characters, right away as my thank you gift for choosing to hang out with me.

Once Upon a Star

A high school crush....

Blake was a nerd in high school. Never noticed. Looked over. So, it was no wonder that Audrey paid no attention to him, but now that she's back in town...

Audrey left Star Lake to pursue acting, but when she ends up pregnant and alone, she finds herself forced to return home.

Can Blake show Audrey a new side? Will she trust him enough to stay?

Read on for a taste of Once Upon a Star....

18

ONCE UPON A STAR PREVIEW

Audrey tried to peek around the nurses leaning over the silver table, obscuring the view of the thing she wanted to see most.

"Are you ready, Mom?" The head nurse, a kind, older woman with just a touch of gray in her dark hair, turned to Audrey, a tiny blue package in her arms.

Mom. The word had never applied to her, and she wasn't sure it fit. Was she ready? Probably not. Would she ever be completely ready? Probably not. But that didn't change reality. She tucked a strand of blond hair behind her ear and nodded.

"Here's your son." The nurse held the swaddled bundle out to her. Audrey opened her hands, unsure of what the nurse wanted her to do. The nurse's face softened and her warm brown eyes sparkled. With one hand, she adjusted Audrey's arms to place the tiny bundle in them. "Hold him like this." She demonstrated the proper technique. "You always want to support his head."

Audrey nodded, trying to keep her arms from shaking. She was afraid to breathe, afraid to move, but mostly afraid she'd drop the infant, so she kept her eyes glued to him. Would he shatter like a piece of glass? The image sent a shiver down her spine. She didn't want to find out.

The nurse's eyes twinkled as she watched Audrey adjust and readjust her holding position. "There is a bassinet here." She pointed at a clear plastic tub that looked like a large shoe box on top of a wheeled table. It didn't look comfortable to Audrey, and she wondered how a baby slept in it. "If you want to take him walking, you need to put him in the bassinet, okay?"

"Do I hold him the rest of the time?" As much as she was enjoying the baby in her arms, what happened when she needed to sleep or use the bathroom?

The woman chuckled. "You hold him as much as you want and put him down when you need a break. We'll come in every few hours to check on you, and we'll show you how to change his diaper and dress him. You'll be a pro before you know it. Don't worry." She patted Audrey's arm like her grandmother used to when she asked a silly question, and then the nurse walked out of the room, still smiling and shaking her head.

Audrey's eyes dropped to the sleeping baby. His shock of dark hair reminded her of his father, the olive-skinned Italian who had charmed her with his fast tongue. She hoped it was the only trait Cayden would get from him. The world didn't need another heart-breaker. "I have no idea what we'll do, Cayden, but we'll figure something out."

BLAKE TURNED the glass on the countertop and glanced up at Max who leaned against the back counter, arms folded across his chest as if he were waiting for the answer to a question. The green of his plaid shirt matched the faded ball cap turned backwards on his head. "Sorry, did you say something? I'm distracted; it's just getting close to Christmas, and I miss Connie." A vision of the day she left popped into his head.

Blake opened the door, expecting to see Connie on the other side in her Sunday best. The church service started in half an hour. Though Connie stood there, his smile faded as he took in her jeans and t-shirt. There was no requirement of the patrons to dress up, but Connie always wore a dress or skirt. "What's going on?" Blake asked.

Connie bit her lip and her eyes fell to the ground. "I wanted to say goodbye."

"Goodbye?"

"I can't stay any longer, Blake." Her eyes lifted to meet his, and he saw the shimmer of liquid in them. "I hoped I could make a life here, but I'm a city girl. I miss the lights and night life. I miss the excitement."

"But, we were discussing marriage last week." Blake struggled to make her words compute in his brain.

"I know," she nodded, "and that's what got me thinking. The thought of living the rest of my life here is depressing, so though I love you, I have to say goodbye." She leaned in and pecked his cheek before flashing a sad smile and walking back to her car.

With a heavy heart, Blake watched her drive away before shutting the door and leaning against it. His brain tried to make sense of her departure.

"I get it," Max said, leaning forward and dispersing Blake's memory. "It's not the same, but you're welcome to spend Christmas with Layla and me.

Blake offered a half smile. "I'll consider it, but it's your first Christmas together. You've been in love with that woman since I've known you and I don't want to be a third wheel. Besides, I'll probably hit the Christmas Eve service at church and spend the day with my mom. She's been lonely without my father around."

Max shrugged and turned back to the kitchen to finish serving the lunch crowd.

Blake took a bite of his hamburger, but while he knew it was delicious—Max was known for his burgers—it held no taste in his current mood. He fished a few dollars out of his wallet, laid the money on the counter, picked up his coat, and walked out the door.

The McAllister development where he worked sat a mile up the road, but as he still had fifteen minutes remaining on his lunch break, he decided to walk through downtown. His own house resided on the quiet outskirts of town, so other than hanging out with Max at The Diner, he didn't spend much time in the downtown area.

Blake pulled his coat tighter as the winter air bit through the heavy wool. Star Lake generally received one or two good snowfalls every winter, and though Christmas was still a few weeks away, the chill in the air made him believe the first snow was coming.

He didn't mind the snow, but he enjoyed it more when he had someone to share the experience with. Curling in front of the fireplace alone held little appeal.

~

AUDREY SHOVED the last item in her suitcase and pushed down on the bulging bag as she tugged on the zipper.

"Where are you going to go?" Desiree asked, leaning against the doorframe.

Desiree was Audrey's roommate, and the two were about as different as night and day. Where Audrey was pale and blond, Desiree had darker skin and long dark hair.

"The only place I can," Audrey said with a sigh. "Home."

The thought held little appeal. Her wealthy parents had given her access to her trust fund at eighteen, and Audrey had opted to move to LA to try her hand at acting. At first, it had been fun. She'd found a few jobs and been in a few commercials, but then the jobs had become fewer and farther between, and after she ended up pregnant, they had dried up completely. Now all the money she had saved was almost gone.

Desiree's nose scrunched in disgust. "You'd go back to that tiny town, why?"

"I haven't had a job in months Dez, my savings have run out, and I can't go to work without someone to watch Cayden. If I go home, I can get help from my parents until I get back on my feet."

At least she hoped they would help. They hadn't been too happy when she decided not to go to college, but she didn't think they would turn their grandson away, even if they didn't want to help her.

Desiree shrugged and flicked her hair behind her bony shoulder. "Nothing in the world would make me return to my crappy hometown."

Audrey knew Desiree's home life had been rough, but while she hadn't wanted to grow up under her mother's thumb, it hadn't been a bad childhood. "I don't know if I'll ever be back, but I wish you luck."

After a quick hug, Audrey picked up Cayden's car seat, slung her bag over her shoulder, and left the apartment she had called home for the last few years.

Click here to sign up for my newsletter and continue reading Once Upon a Star.

WOULD YOU LEAVE A REVIEW?

As an author, I highly appreciate the feedback I get from my readers. It helps others make an informed decision before buying my book. If you enjoyed this book, please review at your retailer.

If you would like to know what happens to the third robber, join my newsletter for more of the Sage Creek Saga.

Do you like free books? I'm offering a free sample of my next book Free Sample!

THE STORY DOESN'T END!

You've met a few people and fallen in love….

I bet you're wondering how you can meet everyone else.

Star Lake Series:

When Love Returns: The first in the Star Lake series. Presley Hays and Brandon Scott were best friends in High School until Morgan entered their town and stole Brandon's heart. Devastated, Presley takes a scholarship to Le Cordon Bleu, but five years later, she is back in Star Lake after a tough breakup. Brandon thought he'd never return to Star Lake after Morgan left him and his daughter Joy, but when his father needs help, he returns home and finds more than he bargained for. Can Presley and Brandon forget past hurts or will their stubborn natures keep them apart forever?

Once Upon a Star: The second book in the Star Lake series. Audrey left Star Lake to pursue acting, but after an unplanned pregnancy her jobs and her money dwindled, leaving her no option except to return home and start over. Blake was the quintessential nerd in high school and was never able to tell Audrey how he felt. Now that he's gained confidence and some muscle, will he finally be able to reveal his feelings? Once Upon a Star will take you back to Christmas in Star Lake. Revisit your favorite characters and meet a few ones in this sweet Christmas read.

Love Conquers All: Lanie Perkins Hall never imagined being divorced at thirty. Nor did she imagine falling for an old friend, but when she runs into Azarius Jacobson, she can't deny the attraction. As they begin to spend more time together, Lanie struggles with the fact Azarius keeps his past a secret. What is he hiding? And will she ever be able to get him to open up? Azarius Jacobson has loved Lanie Perkins Hall from the moment he saw her, but issues from his past have left him guarded. Now that he has another chance with her, will he find the courage to share his life with her? Or will his emotional walls create a barrier that will leave him alone once more? Find out in this heartfelt, emotional third book (stand alone) in the Star Lake series.

The Heartbeats Series:

Where It All Began: Sandra Baker thought her life was on the right track until she ended up pregnant. Her boyfriend, not wanting the baby, pushes her to have an abortion. After the procedure, Sandra's life falls apart, and she turns to alcohol. Her relationship ends, and she struggles to find meaning in her life. When she meets Henry Dobbs, a strong Christian man, she begins to wonder if God would accept her. Will she tell Henry her darkest secret? And will she ever be able to forgive herself and find healing? Find out in this emotional love story.

The Power of Prayer: Callie Green thought she had her whole life planned out until her fiance left her at the altar. When her carefully laid plans crumble, she begins to make mistakes at work and engage in uncharacteristic activities. After a mistake nearly costs her her job, she cashes in her honeymoon tickets for some time away. There she meets JD, a charming Christian man who, even though she is not a believer, captures her interest. Before their relationship can deepen, Callie's ex-fiance shows back up in her life and she is forced to choose between Daniel and JD. Who will she choose and how will her choice affect the rest of her life? Find out in this touching novel.

When Hearts Collide: Amanda Adams has always been a Christian, but she's a novice at relationships. When she meets Caleb, her emotions get the best of her and she ignores the sign that something is amiss. Will she find out before it's too late? Jared Masterson is still healing from his girlfriend's strange rejection and disappearance when he meets Amanda. She captivates his heart, but can he save her from making the biggest mistake of her life? A must read for mothers and daughters. Though part of the series and the first of the college spin off series, it is a stand alone book and can be read separately.

A Past Forgiven: Jess Peterson has lived a life of abuse and lost her self worth, but when she is paired with a Christian roommate, she begins to wonder if there is a loving father looking down on her. Her decisions lead her one way, but when she ends up pregnant, she must make some major changes. Chad Michelson is healing from his own past and uses meaningless relationships to hide his pain, but when Jess becomes pregnant, he begins to wonder about the meaning of life. Can he step up and be there for Jess and the baby?

Sweet Billionaires Series:

The Billionaire's Secret: Maxwell Banks was the

ultimate player until he found himself caring for a daughter he didn't know he had. Can he change to become the role model she needs? Alyssa Miller hasn't had the best luck with past relationships, so why is she falling for the one man who is sure to break her heart? Though nearly complete opposites, feelings develop, but can Max really change his philandering ways? Or will one mistake seal his fate forever?

A Brush with a Billionaire: Brent just wanted to finish his novel in peace, but when his car breaks down in Sweet Grove, he is forced to deal with a female mechanic and try to get along. Sam thought she had given up on city boys, but when Brent shows up in her shop, she finds herself fighting attraction. Will their stubborn natures keep them apart or can a small town festival bring them together?

The Billionaire's Christmas Miracle: Drew Devonshire is captivated by the woman he meets at a masquerade ball, but who is she? Gwen Rodgers is a teacher, but when she pretends to be her friend and meets Drew at a masquerade ball, her world gets thrown upside down.

The Billionaire's Cowboy Groom: Carrie Bliss finally found the man she wants to marry but there's just one little problem. She's technically still married. Cal Roper hasn't seen her in years but his heart still belongs to his wife. When she returns to town requesting a divorce, can he convince her they belong together?

The Lawkeeper Series:

Lawfully Matched: Kate Whidby doesn't want to impose on her newly married brother after their parents die, so she accepts a mail order bride offer in the paper. Little does she know the man she intends to marry has a dark past, sending her fleeing into a neighboring town and into Jesse Jenning's life. Jesse never wanted to be in law enforcement, but after a band of robbers kills his fiancee, he dons the badge and swears revenge. Will he find his fiancee's killer? And when Kate flies into his life, will he be able to put his painful past behind him in order to love again?

Lawfully Justified: William Cook turns to bounty hunting after losing his wife. When he suffers a life-threatening injury, he is forced to stay in town with an intriguing woman. Emma Stewart has moved back in with her widowed father, the town doctor, but she still longs for a family of her own, so no one is more surprised than she is when she starts to develop feeling for the bounty hunter, who hides his heart of gold behind a rugged exterior. Can Emma offer William a reason to stay? Can William find a way to heal from his broken past to start a future with Emma? Or will a haunting secret take away all the possibilities of this budding romance?

The Scarlet Wedding: William and Emma are planning their wedding, but an outbreak and a return from his past force them to change their plans. Is a happily ever after still in their future?

Lawfully Redeemed: Dani Higgins is a K9 cop looking to make a name for herself, but she finds herself at the mercy of a stranger after an accident. Calvin Phillips just wanted to help his brother, but somehow he ended up in the middle of a police investigation and caring for the woman trying to bring his brother in.

Lawfully Pursued: SWAT Officer Jesse Calhoun wasn't looking for love, much less with a billionaire's daughter, but Brie is hard to ignore. Brie Carter was just looking for a little fun but when a bet goes wrong, how does she keep from losing the man she's fallen in love with?

The Still Small Voice Series:

The Still Small Voice: Jordan Wright was searching for something after she gave her son up for adoption. What she found was God, and she began receiving visions. But can she trust Him when he asks her to do something big? Kat Jameson had long been a luke-warm Christian, but when her friend dies and she begins seeing lights, she thinks she is going crazy. Then she meets someone with a message for her. Will she be able to give up control and do what is asked of her?

A Spark in the Darkness coming soon!

Blushing Brides Series:

The Cowboy's Reality Bride: Tyler Hall just wanted to find love, but the women he dated wanted more than his small-town life provided. He gets more than he bargained for when he ends up on a reality dating show and falls for a woman who is not a contestant. Laney Swann has been running from her past for years, but it takes meeting a man on a reality dating show to make her see there's no need to run.

The Reality Bride's Baby: Laney wants nothing more than a baby, but when she starts feeling dizzy is it pregnancy or something more serious?

The Producer's Unlikely Bride: Justin Miller had given up on love, but when his image needs help, he finds himself needing the aid of a stranger who just happens to be a romance writer. Ava McDermott is waiting for the perfect love, but after agreeing to a fake relationship with Justin, she finds herself falling for real.

The Soldier's Steadfast Bride: coming soon

The Cop's Fiery Bride: coming soon

Stand Alones:

Love Renewed: This books is part of the multi author second chance series. When fate reunites high school sweethearts separated by life's choices, can they find a second chance at love at a snowy lodge amid a little mystery?

Her children's early reader chapter book series:

The Wishing Stone #1: Dangerous Dinosaur

The Wishing Stone #2: Dragon Dilemma

The Wishing Stone #3: Mesmerizing Mermaids

The Wishing Stone #4: Pyramid Puzzle

The Wishing Stone Inspirations 1: Mary's Miracle

authorloranahoopes.com

loranahoopes@gmail.com

To see a list of all her books

authorloranahoopes.com

loranahoopes@gmail.com

ABOUT THE AUTHOR

Lorana Hoopes is an inspirational author originally from Texas but now living in the PNW with her husband and three children. When not writing, she can be seen kickboxing at the gym, singing, or acting on stage. One day, she hopes to retire from teaching and write full time.